A Love Unresolved

VEDANSH SINGH

ISBN 979-8-89610-376-9

About the Author

Vedansh Singh Rajput is a debut author with a specialization in Sports and a Bachelor's degree in the field of sports. His passion for weaving compelling stories that explore the complexities of human emotions and relationships is a culmination of his first novel. A lifelong reader of historical fiction, he draws inspiration from his travels and the diverse cultures he has encountered. Born and raised in Madhya Pradesh, Vedansh now resides in his hometown where he continues to write and immerse himself in the world of literature along with his business. "A Love Unresolved", his first novel, is a journey into the heart of resilience and self-discovery, making it engaging and approachable for readers. When he's not writing, Vedansh enjoys hiking, and reading, and is a loner.

Vedansh personally is a man who tries not to compromise with his morals. He is morally zealous rather one can say. He loves animals, He has a small circle of friends but is deeply invested with who he has. For him, his commitments and his words value more than anything else.

*In your eyes, I see the reflection of a love
that knows no boundaries – pure, passionate,
and eternal."*

Contents

Contents

Chapter 1

World of Wishes

---✤✤---

Nahar, started from home with mixed feelings of hope, anxiety and bewilderment. Through his journey to the coaching which he has joined recently, on his first day, he wondered if he could succeed for the road taken towards his goals and dreams. Trees passing by felt to him as if they were all wishing him a good luck for his dreams. Nahar has always been an introvert with an affirm conduct in his behaviour. And now it was to be seen if he could make any friends there and gel up well with them. To his and everyone's surprise he was able to do so. In a few days of interaction, he made into his own cocoon with his selective ones. So determined, so focussed he started his preparations that, many thought he would really make up to his dreams. He started with a good pace and was going well, managing both the spheres of his exam and his coaching's.

Classes in the first half and rest would be the library he would spend his time and this was his regular job now. An early stepping stone to his dreams were now engraving his life's journey. So sincere and disciplined he managed himself to be. Everything was on its own pace with beautiful memories imprinting his life experiences.

His journey throughout the preparation becomes a roller coaster ride to him. As he deals with tons of emotions there, fighting his inner self with so many challenges, somewhere insecurities of not being able to do good and enough satisfying for him and his family, sounding so much of a typical Indian family.

India is an extremely pronatalist society, and the desire to have a male child is greatly stressed and is considered by some to be a man's highest duty, a religious necessity, and a source of emotional and familial gratification and as a consequence, this love of theirs get transform into pillars of hopes, expectations and presumptions that often results into a distorted emotional break between them.

Nahar too was under the same roof of surmise and conjecture.

Chapter 2

Familiar in goals

N ahar marked it a point to do his best and to prove himself as early as possible. He couldn't afford a long period of time wasting in his preparations. He wanted to bring out the result for him as soon as possible. His self-respect was so entangled into ego that he couldn't be dependent on his family for long. It was a great positive signal which added a fuel to his motivation to achieve great in his life. Doing a 9 to 6 job he felt wasn't his cup of tea. He always saw himself in uniform with an officer grade opportunity. So, he made himself involved so much into his studies that he had no time for other stuffs which could hinder his preparations. His days were structured around his studies and his free time was spent with his friends - Ragini, Sudiksha, Ruhi and Adesh, people he met at the coaching with the same sense of spirit as him. They shared the similar goals and their bond was built on mutual support. The group would often meet at the library, combined study sessions followed with moments of laughter and friendship flourished like a bloom in their garden. Nahar was experiencing a new-found happiness, joy and contentment in his life. He was getting fond of his people as in no time they all became like the members of the same family. There was an unspoken understanding between them that they were all in this together, helping each other whenever someone felt stuck or demotivated. Adesh, being the more easy-going one, would often lighten the mood, when the stress of exams became overburdened. He had a way of making even the tensest moments feel bearable with his jokes and laid-back attitude. Everyone, each step ahead was fixed with their aims and objectives. They laughed and eased themselves with frequent breaks without forgetting the goal they were here for, a zeal of enthusiasm in all young minds and the spirit of achieving something really great. Greater than they could think of, bigger than their families could dream of and it was progressively going well.

Chapter 3

Affinity Towards

By this time Nahar developed a profound impact of Ruhi in his life. Ruhi was a bit different than others. Different as in, an elder to all, with a limiting factor in her life as something very indifferently was chasing her and she was before it as if it toggled her. But as destined, a different table was already booked for her and she had to move somewhere else with unspun dreams leaving behind.

Ruhi preoccupied so much into herself and her preparations, so least bothered was she that morning her classes and afternoon the library kept her fully engaged. A devoted time towards her studies was her entire day's target. Though completely drowned in her studies she remained but she made it a note to attend to those whoever came to her with doubts or confusions, wholeheartedly as she had been experienced and wise enough to guide others, especially to those who were the freshers in this preparation. He was told by one of his mentors to take help from her in case of any doubt and thus, Nahar had developed an affinity towards her. This led-to-bond between both made their relation strong and defined.

Their track of Nahar from "Hi Dii" to "Dii, come I'll drop you" grew so strong that Nahar became quite comfortable and ease going in the coaching with days passing. Now Nahar would study, research over his plans and made strategies getting involved so nicely with the studies. This brought a soothing satisfaction to Nahar as he was doing that, what he came here for and because in this Ruhi became that one factor who brought a sense of security and contentment in Nahar's life, he got a go to person to his problems and insecurities he would share with.

Chapter 4

Filling Gaps

——◆◆——

Ruhi in that meantime managed with something that could again keep her going as it did to her previously and as a result she had to leave and move on to another place by now. It was both a cause for celebration and a bittersweet moment for the group. She tried her best to fit in but life had different plans for her. And one day with all her stuff packed and done she was ready to move to another city she had got the opportunity from. The group threw her a small farewell party, reminiscing about all the times they had spent studying together. Ruhi with her calm and determined nature, had been a steady presence in the group. Her leaving felt like the end of an era for them. People come and go with time and so was Ruhi gone. Occupied in the new space and work culture Ruhi became that rare element which was stable but least reactive. With Ruhi's experience everybody learnt to have to be more punctual and more promising towards each one's goal. A void being created, everybody again accelerated their studies with more fuel to reach to their destinations.

With Ruhi gone, Nahar noticed a subtle shift in the group dynamic. Though they still studied together, something felt missing. He started spending more time alone at the library, pushing himself harder to fill the gap left by Ruhi's absence. As Nahar immersed himself more in his studies, he began to feel the loneliness creeping in, despite the presence of his remaining friends. Ruhi's departure had left an emotional void, and Nahar realized he missed having someone to confide in, someone who understood him on a deeper level.

Ragini and Sudiksha, though supportive, were also busy with their own preparations. Their conversations remained focused on exams and study material, but the deeper connection Nahar craved was missing.

This emotional state is what made Nahar more prone to emotional breakdown. As a result, unknowingly, he became deficient of human support and care. This incompleteness in something being unable to share and talk paved a way towards something unusual to his nature. He didn't realize it at that time, but he was ready for someone new to fill that emotional space and Milli, with her warmth and charm, fit right in. He welcomed this new-found bond with great love, care and concern which he thought that would bring him peace and love in his life.

Chapter 5

The Stand In

———◆◆———

(*The Library Encounter*) The library was that space of the coaching institute where Nahar studied for his exams. It was a peaceful place, filled with the soft rustling of papers and the hum of students absorbed in their work. Nahar was regular here, who often came after his classes to study in silence. The library is quiet, with long rows of desks, tall bookshelves, and a large window that lets in natural light. The smell of old books fills the air, and the only sounds are the turning of pages and the occasional soft conversation between students.

Nahar now trying to be more focussed is seated at his usual spot in the corner, surrounded by notes and textbooks. He's deeply focused into his studies, preparing for an upcoming exam. He's a diligent student, someone who values his time and prefers the calmness of the library.

(*A Glance at the Door*): As Nahar flips through his notes, the door to the library opens, and Milli walks in. She's unfamiliar to him, someone he hasn't seen before in the library, and she instantly catches his attention. Milli walks in, carrying few books, looking slightly lost as she searches for a place to sit. She's new to the coaching centre, maybe recently enrolled, and she's trying to find her way around. Her eyes scan the room, and she notices Nahar sitting alone. She's dressed casually, with her hair pulled back, looking studious but with a warmth in her demeanour. There's a lightness about her, a sense of curiosity and calm, even in this serious academic setting.

The library was unusually full that day, with hardly any vacant seats. Milli looks around, hesitating, and then spots the empty one lying beside Nahar. She approaches, a little shy but determined. She leans forward slightly and softly asks, "Is this seat taken?" Her voice is polite, with a hint of nervousness. Nahar looks up, a bit surprised but in no time, he offers her the seat with a small smile. "No, it's all yours," he says, moving some of his books aside to make room for her.

Studying in Silence, for the first few minutes, they don't speak. Milli takes out her books and starts to read, while Nahar continues with his work. There's a comfortable silence between them, but Nahar can't help but steal occasional glances at her. He notices the way she quietly focuses on her work, how her eyes scan the pages with determination. There's something intriguing about her, though he can't quite put his finger on it yet.

Chapter 6

Found Interest

(Now Nahar Notices Milli More Often)

Frequent Encounters make Nahar more infatuated towards her personality now. After their initial meeting in the library, Nahar begins noticing Milli more frequently. She is present in the library during breaks, between coaching classes. Each time he sees her, he feels a slight flutter of excitement. Subtle Observations engraving Nahar's mind makes him more and more inclined towards her. He starts paying attention to little details about Milli—the way she tucks her hair behind the ear when she's reading, her habit of scribbling notes in the margins of her textbooks, or how she always carries a water bottle with her. Each moment passing brings an unconscious attraction that entangles Nahar making him feel more and more likeliness towards her. Though he's not fully aware of it, he is developing a feeling like that of a crush on her. He finds himself looking for her in the library or hoping to bump into her during his breaks. It's becoming a distraction, but not once he minds that of a much. While all of this play Ragini's Observation bring him a holdback for a while. During one of their group study sessions, Ragini is the first to notice Nahar's wandering attention. He's supposed to be focused on his notes, but his eyes keep drifting to the entrance of the library, where Milli usually enters.

With a known familiar smile, Ragini nudges Nahar. "Looking for someone, Nahar? Or are you just memorizing the library's entrance?" in the meantime Adesh joins in. Adesh, ever the joker, picks up on Ragini's teasing. "I don't know, Ragini, maybe he's got a special study guide coming through that door," he says with a wink, making everyone laugh. While Ragini and Adesh tease him, Sudiksha, who's always been the sincerest one in the group, just gives Nahar an amused smile. She's seen the way Nahar looks at Milli, but she doesn't say much—just gives him a supportive nod when the teasing gets too much.

Playful embarrassment surrounds Nahar and leaves him numbed at times by now with his friends noticing his every move with his increasingly grown interest in someone. As Nahar has always been the boy with stern attitude towards few things he was so particular about. The boy with so few selected interactions, nobody thought or ever imagined this kind of change can cause so much of an alteration in his behaviour that too in this manner.

Often though slightly embarrassed by the teasing, Nahar couldn't help but smile. "It's not like that," he tried against but the slight redness in his cheeks gave him away. His friends knew him so well.

Denial and Deflection was one-way Nahar could choose to escape the teasing. He tried to divert the conversation back to studying. "Let's just focus on the book, okay? It's more important than... whatever you're thinking." And in reply Adesh's retort left him again on the same ground. "Sure, sure. But when you need help studying her phone number, let me know," Adesh adds with a grin, earning more laughter from the group. Coincidence plays its part well and the timing was so punctually driven that as if on cue, Milli walks into the library just as Nahar is trying to brush off the teasing. His friends exchange knowing looks, and Nahar tries (and fails) to hide his flustered expression. Nahar's nervousness makes him feel his heart skip a beat when Milli smiles in his direction. With so many certain behavioural changes in Nahar Ragini's and Adesh's ongoing teasing takes sparks. As Milli settles into her seat, Ragini leans closer to Nahar and whispers, "You should ask her to study with us. Maybe she'll help you focus more." Adesh, always the instigator, adds, "Or maybe she'll be more of a distraction—either way, it'll be fun to watch." Nahar with an embarrassed smile flustered but secretly enjoying the attention, just shakes his head. "You guys are impossible," he mutters, though there's a smile tugging at his lips. Despite the teasing, he can't help but think about what it would be like to get to know Milli better.

Chapter 7

Valentine's Day

Nahar's Plan to Invite Milli for Breakfast

{It's quoted so well and fits so meaningfully in case of Nahar, "Love is more than longing gazes". Nahar had obsessively grown so fond of the girl that he chooses valentine's day to take his steps to another level. Nahar, at variance to his nature was into something that was so different and challenging for him, he was unaware with.}

Study Sessions are on its pace and there comes a day to again instigate something unusual with Nahar which he isn't able to stop thinking about. It's Valentine's Day and while the world outside is filled with couples exchanging flowers and chocolates, Nahar, Adesh, and Sudiksha are doing what they always do—group study. They're in class surrounded by textbooks and notes trying to stay focused.

(*Nahar's Distraction*), Nahar can't help but feels restless. It's Valentine's day after all and despite trying to stay focused on his studies, his mind keeps wandering back to Milli. He glances out from the window of the classroom, his eyes looking out for the one he would like to have his day spent.

(moment as Milli arrives),

Just as Nahar is about to turn back to his notes, he catches the sight of Milli walking into the library. She is dressed casually, carrying her books, looking like she's ready for another day of studying. But for Nahar, seeing her is like the green light radiating, which signals people to head towards their final destination.

(Insight) Why *not?* Nahar thinks to himself. *It's Valentine's Day. Why shouldn't I do something special?* He smiles to himself, a plan already framed in his mind pretending to himself as if nothing wrong was he doing as its normal to have a small plan with anyone randomly without having any expectations or feeling like that of conservatives who can't meet or have a cup of coffee on this very special day. Making his head clear with this pseudo-satisfaction he collects his strength to execute to what he as planned or is planning towards.

Convincingly preaching Sudiksha Nahar leans towards her who's seated next to him, her face buried in textbook. "Hey, Sudiksha," he whispers and nudges her. She looks up, slightly confused. "What's up?" she asks

Nahar although with the very known intuition that he's going to talk about. Nahar grins, asking her a favour.

(*Nahar to Sudiksha*): "just look at Milli over there, he says with a gesture towards the library. Sudiksha with a frown on her forehead, already suspecting what Nahar is about to suggest.

"I was thinking...how nice it would be if you invite her to have breakfast with us? You know, Just in a very casual manner." Sudiksha gives him a look that's a mix of amusement and disbelief. "Are you serious? You want me to ask her to have breakfast with us, that too on an occasion of such an obvious day, on "Valentine's Day?" Nahar seemingly so obsessed and overtly expressive which actually wasn't his behaviour was such an unbelievable and surprising fact to Sudiksha, was trying to play it cool.

"Yeah, just as friends. There's nothing so odd about it. It'll be fun!" He says to her being so hopeful and waiting to her agreement. And thus, to his very good friend, not letting him upset with her disagreement Sudiksha after a moment of hesitation, sighs and says the final Yes, "Fine, I'll do it. But only because it's you, and you're terribly being so stupid at this kind of thing," she teases, grabbing her bag.

Nahar beams, grateful. "You're the best," he says, his excitement barely contained. As Sudiksha gets up, Nahar watches her heading towards the library, his heart racing in anticipation.

(Nahar's Nervousness and floating butterflies in him)

Sudiksha walks away, Nahar can't help but feel a mix of excitement and nervousness. He tries to focus on the study material in front of him, but his mind is completely occupied by thoughts of Milli and how this breakfast invitation might go.

Meanwhile Adesh who has been observing the whole exchange, gives Nahar a familiar look. "Valentine's Day breakfast, huh? Bold move," he says with a grin. Nahar just shrugs, trying to act casual. "It's just breakfast. No big deal," he says, though his expression betrays his nerves.

As planned Sudiksha approaches Milli with a friendly smile. She sits beside her pretending to be normally going and sitting out there, "Hey, Milli! We're just about to take a break from studies and have some breakfast. You should join us." Milli' hesitatingly! looks up slowly closing her book, momentarily surprised by the invitation. She being amazed for a moment, glancing back at her study materials says, "Breakfast, huh? I don't know, I was planning to study a bit more..." she trails off.

Sudiksha, not wanting to let the moment go out of track, smiles and tries to reconvince her. "Come on, it'll be quick and we'll return in a short while, (*letting not a single chance for Milli to deny*). Just a small break to recharge.

Besides, it's Valentine's Day—everyone deserves a little treat, right?" Sudiksha sounding more like that of Nahar, tries to convince Milli.

After a moment's thought, Milli nods and smiles agreeing to the proposal offered by Sudiksha. She keeps back the books into her bag. Sudiksha's expression of achieving victory was a sort of fun. She stands up as Milli gathers her things, feeling a bit proud that she was able to carry out Nahar's plan smoothly. As soon as Milli is ready, Sudiksha excuses herself to tell Nahar. She exits the library and walks over to where Nahar and Adesh are waiting. Nahar looks at her expectantly, and she smiles, giving him a thumbs-up. "Mission accomplished; she's coming" she says with a big smile on her face, so friendly and so pure. There, Nahar's heart races with excitement, he grins at Sudiksha, feeling a mix of nerves and anticipation. "You're amazing," he says, genuinely appreciative.

Nahar quickly pulls Sudiksha aside and whispers his plan to her. "Okay, so here's what I need you and Adesh to do. After we sit down for breakfast, hang around for a little while. But then, after maybe ten or fifteen minutes later find an excuse to leave. Like just say you forgot something or sort of anything like that."

Sudiksha smirks knowingly. "Ah, I see. You want to have some time alone with her." Nahar nods, helping himself not to blush. "Yeah... I just think it'll be easier to talk if it's just the two of us" he replies. Sudiksha chuckles and pats him on the shoulder saying, "No problem. We'll make ourselves scarce."

(The Breakfast Plan is in Motion) and the group proceeds towards a café for breakfast. The group meets up at a small café near the library. Nahar, Sudiksha, Milli and Adesh reach and have a table for themselves. Milli still looks a little surprised but comfortable. "Thanks for inviting me," she says as she sits down.

Casual conversation transcends among the group over breakfast. At first, they stick to safe topics like studies, coaching classes, and some lighter jokes. Nahar participates in the conversation but is constantly thinking about how to steer it towards more meaningful subjects once Sudiksha and Adesh leave.

Meanwhile Sudiksha and Adesh make themselves ready for an exit and after about fifteen minutes, Sudiksha glances at Adesh, giving him a subtle signal. She then turns to Milli and Nahar pretending to have forgotten something and says "Hey! Adesh, I just remembered that we have to collect a parcel, guys we'll catch you later in about ten to fifteen minutes", saying this they both leave the café creating a space for both of them to have their own time as planned by Nahar. Milli looks slightly surprised but nods. "Oh, okay. No problem." She doesn't seem to suspect anything.

Nahar's inner excitement leaves him puzzled with so much of mixed emotions and feelings, he tries to stay calm, but inside, he's thrilled. Now that it's just him and Milli, he feels the opportunity to finally have that genuine conversation with her. After Sudiksha and Adesh leave, Nahar takes a deep breath. It's just him and Milli now, and he doesn't want to waste the opportunity. He decides to keep things light at first. "So, how's your day going so far?" he asks with a casual smile. Milli smiles back, taking a sip of her tea. "Not too bad. Just the usual—studying, trying to stay focused." She laughs softly. "What about you? I noticed, you always seem pretty focused in the library." Nahar chuckles, "Yeah, well, I try but some days, it's harder than others." He pauses for a moment before adding, "Like today."

(Digging deeper into interests)

Wanting to know more about her, Nahar trying to be more casual and normal, further adds to the conversation. "So, what do you do when you're not studying? Any hobbies or things you enjoy apart from studies and books?" Milli tilts her head thoughtfully and replies, "Well, one thing I love is playing chess. It's like a mental workout—it keeps me calm and focused." Nahar's eyes widen in surprise. "Oh really" (to his surprise as he also was so fond of it), I love chess too. I used to play with my friends all the time during college days he says. It's really a game of strategy."

Connecting with similar fondness and enjoying the synced habits they both laugh and there's a moment of mutual appreciation for their shared interest. Nahar is thrilled—he hadn't expected to find something so specific in common with her.

(*Discovering a bigger Connection: Army Aspirations*)

The conversation flows naturally as they move from chess to their future aspirations. Nahar is curious. "So, what are you studying for? You seem pretty determined." Milli's expression turns more serious but passionate. "I'm preparing for the army entrance exam. It's something I've wanted for a long time. I really want to serve."

(Nahar in complete surprise and admiration; genuinely impressed utters seemingly so glad and corelating),

"The army? That's amazing. I'm preparing for the same thing. I've always felt this strong sense of duty to serve. It's not just a career—it's a calling, right?"

(Milli smiling to his words), her eyes light up as she nods in agreement. "Exactly! It's about being part of something bigger than yourself, something that truly matters. Not everyone understands that." She looks at

Nahar with newfound respect, realizing they share more than just a casual interest.

(Mutual Admiration brings an added flavour to their conversation)

As they continue talking about their aspirations, Nahar feels a deeper connection building in between them. It's not just about shared hobbies anymore—they both have similar goals and values, which makes the conversation feel more meaningful paving a way stronger towards Nahar's defined goals.

(Sudiksha's Check-In)

Suddenly, Nahar's phone vibrates with a message from Sudiksha. He checks it under the table, smiling when he sees her text: *Everything okay?*

Nahar in response quickly texts back, "*All good. You can come back in a few minutes*". Meanwhile he glances up at Milli, making sure she doesn't notice too much and slips his phone back into his pocket.

(Seeing the situation getting to wind up, Nahar diverts wrapping up the conversation)

After a few more minutes of talking about everything from the pressure of preparing for the entrance exams to their favourite books, Nahar sees Sudiksha and Adesh returning to the table.

Nahar being satisfied with the conversation is glad that not only did he learn more about Milli, but he also felt a genuine connection forming between them. He hopes this is the start of something more, something deeper, something so genuine.

Chapter 8

The Close In

The Chess Games and Chai Conversations (Finding Time to Play): After that long breakfast conversation, Nahar and Milli's connection was flourishing and they were moving a step ahead in the affair they were engaged in. Whenever they got free time, in between study sessions, they met for a swift game of chess. It started becoming their shared activity, something they both awaited with pleasure.

Friendly Competition promotes that space for each other where they both tried could fit in. Their games are competitive but friendly. Sometimes Milli wins, sometimes Nahar, but the banter is always light-hearted. "You always think three steps ahead," Milli teases after losing a game. Nahar grins, "It's all about strategy, right? Just like life."

(Chai After Chess)

After their chess games, it becomes a habit for them to head to a nearby tea stall for chai. These chai breaks provide them right set of circumstances for cavernous conversations - about life, yearning and sometimes even their memoirs.

During this whole tittle-tattle time, Nahar's feelings brighten up more thoroughly. For Nahar, these moments meant that of a voluptuous bosom. As they take a sip of tea and talk, he starts realizing that he's falling for Milli. Her smile, her intelligence, her passion for the army—all of it pulls him in and directs him towards that empty space in his life which has brought him to a monotonous way of living since back days. Now he is cheerful, happy and more merrily he cherishes those small things in his life which he rather didn't earlier. And all these good changes he feels are the signals of the true love he has been developing for Milli.

Now each and every moment Nahar feels he should spend with Milli should be his own time, his me time with her and if someone in between comes he feels of a hurdle race he has been running but is unable to because of those hurdles.

Sometimes, Milli, feeling comfortable with Nahar's friends, often asks, "Why don't we invite Adesh, Ragini and sudiksha next time? It'll be fun with the five of us."

(Nahar's spontaneous Excuses), Nahar, wanting to keep these moments private, often makes excuses on behalf of others. "They are busy with some extra classes," or "Adesh has some work today."

He tries to manage manipulatively every single moment whenever he feels someone may come and that their conversation towards another level of this likeliness, endearment may impede.

Often people in love forget the existing world around them. And so was Nahar doing. By now he started making his own hive with Milli and as if nobody could enter his space. Slowly he was shifting towards that private association which included only two members within it.

Milli never seems suspicious, trusting Nahar's words, while Nahar secretly feels relieved to have these moments alone with her.

With each game and chai break, their conversation shifts from surface-level topics to more personal matters. Nahar finds himself opening up to Milli in ways he hasn't with anyone else. He feels like he can be himself around her, and it seems like she feels the same way.

But at the same there's an unspoken tension between them, one that's hard to ignore. While neither of them directly talks about their feelings, it's clear in the way they look at each other, the comfortable silences they share, and the way their conversation seem to linger, as if neither wants the moment to end.

37

Chapter 9

Vivifying the Union

The Evening Power Cut: A Serendipitous Moment

(Nahar Studying Alone): It's a calm soothing evening and Nahar is sitting in his cabin, deeply immersed in his study materials. The soft hum of his desk lamp is the only sound in the room.

Suddenly, everything goes dark. The power cuts out without warning and Nahar looks up, slightly startled. He gets up from his seat and heads towards the door wondering if anyone else is stepping out. As Nahar opens the door of his cabin, he steps outside and is greeted by a light breeze and the smell of rain in the air. The sky is a mix of twilight and dark clouds, with just a sign of raindrops falling. Just then, he sees Milli stepping out from the nearby cabin, looking up at the sky with a smile. The winds gently blow her hair, and the soft drizzle adds a certain glow to the scene. "Looks like we've lost power," she says, noticing Nahar.

Nahar smiles back, feeling a sense of calm wash over him. "Yeah, but the weather's making up for it. It's beautiful out here."

(The Weather Enhances the Mood)

Enjoying the Breeze, they both stand under the dim, fading light of the evening. The wind picks up slightly, and the cool breeze makes everything feel magical. The light rain creates an appease rhythm, making their conversation more deep-seated, as if the world outside has melted away. They start talking about all sorts of things—how they both grew up loving the monsoon season, their favourite memories from childhood and how moments like these make life feel special. Nahar feels a deeper connection with Milli as they share more personal stories.

(Exchanging Numbers)

After a while, Nahar hesitates but finally says, "We should keep in touch, you know, outside of the library and chess." Milli looks at him and smiles. "Yeah, I'd like that."

(Passing Phones), Nahar pulls out his phone and Milli hands him hers. In that placid, almost trance-like moment, they exchange numbers. It feels like an unspoken promise, a next step in their forging link.

(Lingering After the Exchange)

After this imparting exchange, they stand for a moment silently admiring the evening. The rain gets a little heavier, and they laugh as they rush to find shelter.

(*Nahar's Inner Thoughts*) As they part ways, Nahar can't help but feel like something significant had just happened. It wasn't just the exchange of numbers—it was the way they connected in the calm of the evening, under the rain and wind, as if the universe was conspiring to bring them closer sounding more like that of *Om Shanti Om!*

That same evening, after they both retreat to their places, Nahar feels a mix of excitement and nervousness. He holds his phone, staring at Milli's contact, wondering how to start and what to say.

(*The First Message*), After a few minutes of indecision, he finally sends a casual message: *"Hope you didn't get too soaked in the rain today. It was nice talking."*

Milli's Quick Reply: To his relief, Milli replies almost instantly: *"Not too bad! I enjoyed it. The weather made everything better, don't you think?"*

This very seem- to- be casual but friendly parley moment allows through regular and recurring exchange of messages.

(*Late-Night Conversations*)

Over the next few days, their texting escalates into late-night phone calls. They talk about everything—from their studies and chess games to their dreams of joining the army.

These conversations reveal versions of their personalities. Milli talks about her family, her fears about the entrance exams, and how she sometimes feels overwhelmed by the pressure.

Nahar opens up about his own struggles, the moments when he doubted his abilities, and how meeting her has given him a sense of balance. Everything he thought which were problems to him were getting sorted and balanced. And this is what love brings from a character of a person. He feels all right, can withstand and deal with any situation because he knows now he has that go to person who he can open about anything to.

These feelings bring them the sense of security demanding the longingness for more time to be spent together. With the comfort of their phone calls, they start meeting more oft outside the library. They go for walks, have chai together, and continue their chess games. Milli sometimes asks if Adesh or others can join them, but Nahar subtly deflects the idea, wanting to secure his time alone with her. He wants his time to be of her's and her time for him, nobody else should enter that zone and that they shouldn't be involved in.

(Nahar wasn't realising with this preoccupied nature he was somewhere pushing everyone of his own loved ones somewhere away from him. It wasn't affecting them because they were busy watering their own grasses as exams approached near and they didn't forget their aims and objectives and the reason they here for. But for Nahar this all went in delusion and he was into some closemouthed affair entangled completely into.)

But then if this consciousness comes into play then it no longer is love rather becomes a formal exchange and both were not ready for any kind of formal transmission, they were richly and seriously involved into some important affair.

To them the kind of love they were engaged into was setting them free from all the weight and pain in their lives.

Chapter 10

Flames of Obsession

*"**I** fell in love the way you fall asleep: slowly, and then all at once."*

The Idiosyncrasy and Realization of Love

As their bond deepens, Nahar and Milli become inseparable.

Late-Night Confessions: Their phone calls haul long extending till the early hours of the morning. They talk about their dreams, fears, and their future. Sometimes the silence between them feels just as meaningful as the words.

With time, it becomes clear to both Nahar and Milli that what they share is more than friendship. Every touch, every glance lingers longer than necessary. Even when they play chess, their eyes speak what their mouths don't—there's an unspoken understanding that some profound propinquity was germinating.

Small gestures have started to divulge their feelings now. Nahar would casually brush his hand against Milli's or dawdle a little too long when offering her a pen. Milli, reciprocates giving him smiles that light up her entire face and rests her hand on his arm for support when they walk.

(Love in the Air): It's not just them who notice the shift. Their friends begin to see how close they've become. Ragini teases Nahar about how much time he spends with Milli, while Sudiksha sometimes passes deride smiles when Nahar mentions Milli. Even Adesh notices but remains aphonic about it.

(Both Know, But Neither Says It)

(No Formal Confession)- Despite the clear chemistry, neither Nahar nor Milli explicitly say the words "I love you." It's as if they both know it's true, but they're scared to admit it, fearing it might change the dynamic between them.

(The Tension of Unsaid Words): Every meeting, every confabulation surrounds a sense of traction in between. They both know how they feel, but the words hang in the air, unarticulated. Nahar can feel it in the way Milli looks at him, and Milli senses it in Nahar's gesticulation; always protective, always present.

(The Interview and the Gift)

Journey for the Interview as after clearing her first paper, she leaves for the interview round with high hopes. Nahar, Milli's fully supportive, sends her encouraging messages. "You've got this," he texts, "Just be yourself."

(The Waiting Game) - During the interview process, Nahar anxiously waits to hear from her, checking his phone constantly. His heart races each time his phone buzzes, only to find out if it's someone else. The anticipation builds as he imagines how excited Milli will be when she tells him it went well.

(The Heart-breaking Rejection)

The Bad News: Unfortunately, Milli doesn't make it through the interview round. She's rejected. Feeling disappointed and defeated, she heads back home. The rejection stings, but she doesn't let it show when she texts Nahar: *"Didn't make it, but there's always next time."*

(Nahar's Support): Nahar immediately replies, sending her heartfelt words of comfort. "You'll crush it next time, don't worry. I'm still proud of you." He tries to keep her spirits high, not wanting her to feel alone in this.

(Milli's Thoughtful Gesture)

A Gift for Nahar: Even though she's feeling down, Milli stops by a shop on her way home and buys something small for Nahar—a token of affection, something she knows he'll love. She texts him about it: *"Got something for you. Can't wait to show you."*

Nahar's Excitement: Nahar's heart swells with excitement at the thought of receiving a gift from Milli. He's touched that she thought of him even after such a difficult day. Eager to make the moment more personal, he asks her to write his name on the gift. *"That's amazing! You should write my name on it—it'll make it even more special."*

A Symbol of Their Bond: This gift becomes iconic for Nahar. It's more than just a material—it's a reflection of how deep their connection has grown, despite the setbacks they face in their personal lives.

Time and the work affair keep both busy and they are unavailable physically for one another. Distance unites the missing beats of two hearts in love." And this was something being cooked in the relationship between the two were by now deeply in love with each other.

(The Month Apart and the Return Gift)

Milli's Return: After Milli's interview rejection and her so thoughtful frame of mind for Nahar, she eagerly waits to meet him. However, just when she comes back, Nahar has to leave for his college exams. Their plans to meet are postponed, and a month of distance awaits their meeting.

Nahar, fully immersed in his college exams, tries his best to focus on his studies, but thoughts of Milli keep creeping in. Whenever he takes a break, he finds himself checking his phone, scrolling through their old conversations, and thinking about when they'll finally see each other again.

Despite being apart, they stay connected through texts and late-night phone calls. Milli teases him about how long it's taking him to finish his exams, while Nahar playfully complains about how much he misses her chai.

(Nahar's Return Gift)

(The Idea of a Gift): During this distant separation, Nahar reflects on how thoughtful Milli was to buy him a gift after her interview which even didn't go that well as she expected it to go. Wanting to respond earnestly, he spends some time thinking about what would make the perfect return gift.

One day, while shopping after an exam, Nahar spots an elegant pen in a store—a sleek, classy design that would complement formal attire. He immediately thinks of Milli, conjuring up her, using it during interviews or study sessions. He decides this is the perfect gift, symbolizing his support for her professional dreams. Nahar (exhilarated) can't wait to give it to her. He imagines the facial gestures of hers when she would see it, hoping the pen will remind her of his constant belief in her abilities, no matter the setbacks.

(The Anticipation of Meeting Again)

As a month apart drags on, both Nahar and Milli eagerly look forward to the day they can finally meet in person again. The exchange of gifts feels emblematic of both the time they've spent apart and the connection they've managed to maintain despite the distance. Every day heads towards their meeting, Nahar holds the pen in his hand, envisioning how the moment will go. He knows the gift is a little treat but it represents the solicitousness they share.

Chapter 11

Erratic Mood Swings

*(T*he Unexpected Conversation)

Late-Night Call One evening, Nahar and Milli are having another one of their late-night phone conversations. The conversation starts like any other—about their day, plans for the future, and how much they miss each other. But something feels off in Milli's tone, a subtle shift that Nahar can't quite place. Milli's Sudden Statement: Out of nowhere, Milli says, *"Why do we talk so regularly? I don't understand why we're doing this."* Nahar's heart skips a beat. He assumes she's hinting at deepening their relationship, thinking that perhaps it's time to define what they mean to each other.

Nahar's Hopeful Misunderstanding: His mind races, and a surge of excitement rises within him. Maybe this is the moment when she'll confess her feelings—finally acknowledging what they both know but haven't said out loud. But before he can respond, Milli continues, her voice colder than before.

(Milli Wants to end things)

The Shock of Rejection: Milli interrupts Nahar's thoughts, saying, *"I think we should stop everything here."* The words hit Nahar like a punch to the gut. He sits in stunned silence, trying to process what she just said. The girl he thought was as obsessed with him as he was with her is now suggesting they end everything.

Nahar's Confusion: Nahar is at a loss for words. His mind is reeling—what had he missed? Everything seemed perfect between them, or so he thought. He tries to respond, but the words stick in his throat. The silence between them grows heavier with each passing second.

(Silence on Both Sides)

A Deafening Silence: Neither of them speaks. The silence on the phone is suffocating, filled with all the things Nahar wants to say but can't. He wants to ask why, but he's too shocked to form the question. Milli, on the other hand, doesn't offer an explanation, leaving Nahar to fill in the blanks himself.

(The Breakdown)

Nahar breaking the silence, after a long, agonizing pause, Nahar can't hold back any longer. His voice trembles as he asks, "Why, Milli? What happened? Why are you doing this?" He feels a wave of confusion and desperation rise within him. His chest tightens, and for the first time, he lets his emotions spill out.

To his own surprise, Nahar begins to cry. Tears roll down his face, and he tries to speak, but his words are broken. It's the first time he's ever cried in front of Milli, and it feels like his world is crashing down around him. *"I don't understand... Why now? I thought everything was going well."* His voice cracks as he speaks. Milli tries to calm him, in a soft response hearing Nahar cry, Milli's tone softens immediately. She hadn't expected this kind of reaction. She gently tries to calm him down, her voice soothing but distant. *"Nahar, please don't cry. It's not that. I just... I don't know how to explain it right now."*

Comfort, but No Clarity: She attempts to reassure him, but her words don't provide the clarity Nahar so desperately seeks. It's as if she's avoiding giving him the real reason, which only makes him feel more lost. *"Everything's going to be fine, okay? Don't cry."* But to Nahar, it feels like a hollow comfort.

(Nahar's Emotional Collapse)

Nahar's struggle giving him the strength to hold himself back, he tries to regain control of his emotions, but the more he thinks about her words, the more confused he becomes. He feels a mixture of heartbreak, frustration, and a sense of betrayal, even though he doesn't yet fully understand why. *"I thought we were... I thought you felt the same way. Why are you pulling away?"* His voice is barely steady.

(A Growing Sense of Helplessness), Nahar's mind races, trying to piece together the situation, but nothing makes sense. He feels utterly powerless, as though the ground beneath him is giving way. *"Did I do something wrong? Tell me, please. I don't know what's happening."*

Milli Calms Nahar, changing the subject, after hearing his emotional breakdown, she quickly changes the subject, steering the conversation away from the sudden tension. She speaks softly, trying to soothe him with lighter topics. *"Let's not think about this right now. We've both been stressed lately. How are your exams going?"*

Her words are gentle but evasive, and though Nahar feels momentarily relieved, something still feels off. Though Milli's attempt to calm him works, Nahar can't help but notice the strange shift in the conversation. He senses that she's avoiding something important, but he doesn't want to push her too hard. He tells himself that maybe she's just overwhelmed.

A Seed of Suspicion, for the first time, makes Nahar feel a pang of doubt about Milli's loyalty. Her sudden distance, the evasive conversation—none of it sits well with him. His mind races through all the moments they've shared, trying to find an explanation for her behaviour. *"Could it be that she's hiding something?"* he wonders, though he tries to shake off the thought.

(Psychological Insight): Nahar, having a deep understanding of psychology, knows how people can sometimes shift their behaviour to suit their own needs. He wonders if Milli is trying to manipulate the situation in a subtle way. Yet, he brushes it off, thinking it could just be his mind playing tricks on him after months of not seeing each other.

Rationalizing her behaviour, Nahar tries to convince himself that the distance between them is the real issue. "It's been months since we've met," he tells himself, "Maybe she's just feeling disconnected because of that." He knows that long periods of separation can create emotional rifts, but deep down, he can't completely churn up the suspicion that something else is going on.

Nahar is battling his inner struggle and continues to overthink the situation, he finds himself caught between trusting Milli and giving in to the creeping doubts that are starting to form. He feels torn, unsure if he's just being paranoid or if there's something more beneath the surface.

Chapter 12

The Reunion

The corporeal vacuum again brings the heart grow enamour of each other.

The long-awaited Meet and Nahar's anticipation after weeks of being apart and the emotional tension from their last conversation, makes him feel a mixture of excitement and nervousness as he prepares to meet Milli. The pen he bought for her is tucked neatly into his pocket, and he wonders how she'll react when she sees it.

(The meeting spot): They decide to meet at their usual café, the same one where they often shared chai. As Nahar enters, he sees Milli sitting by the window, looking up from her phone with a warm smile. His heart skips a beat, but there's also a nagging thought in the back of his mind-remnants of the doubt that lingered after their last phone call.

(The Exchange of Gifts)

Milli is the first to bring out her gift. It's a small box, neatly wrapped. As Nahar opens it, he finds a thoughtful token—a bracelet with a personalized engraving, something that holds special meaning for both of them. Inside the box, he sees his name, just as he had asked. His face lights up as he holds the gift, feeling a connection reignite between them.

With a soft smile, Nahar pulls out the elegant pen he bought for her. He hands it to Milli, explaining that he thought it would be perfect for her future interviews and exams. Milli's eyes widen with appreciation as she takes it, admiring the sleek design. She thanks him, and for a brief moment, all the tension from their previous conversation melts away.

(Catching Up on Life)

Talking about the exams, they settle into an easy conversation. Milli shares how disappointed she was with her interview, but she tries to stay optimistic, talking about how she plans to prepare better for the next one. Nahar, in turn, tells her about his college exams, laughing about the relief of having them finally over.

A Temporary Peace for a while brings the scenario like it's back to normal. They laugh, joke, and reminisce about their long conversations, and Nahar feels reassured. The warmth in Milli's eyes is familiar, and for a moment, he pushes aside the doubts that had been eating at him. Maybe things are finally getting back on track he feels.

Chapter 13

A Night of Drinks

The Late-Night Call: After a day of catching up and feeling like things are finally back to normal, Nahar and Milli find themselves talking late into the night, just like old times. Their conversation flows easily, with laughter and shared stories.

Milli's unexpected request: Out of the blue, Milli suggests they should have a drink together. *"Why don't we have a drink and chill tonight?"* she says with a playful tone. Nahar is caught off guard, but not opposed. He hesitates for a second, but then remembers that he has a bottle already waiting in his room.

(Nahar's Agreement): Going Along with the Plan: Despite the slight surprise, Nahar agrees, thinking it might add some fun to their night. He figures it's just another way for them to relax and bond. "Sure, I've got a bottle right here. Let's do it."

The Mood Shift: As Nahar grabs the bottle, he feels a strange sense of excitement and curiosity. It's not something they've done before, but it feels spontaneous. He pours himself a glass, wondering how the night will unfold.

The Late-Night Invitation

(The Problem with Nahar's Room)

Realizing the Situation, as Nahar prepares to drink, he suddenly remembers the strict rules in his building—girls aren't allowed in the rooms. He chuckles awkwardly and tells Milli, *"Actually, I can't invite you here. The management would lose their minds if they saw you in my room."* There's also no way they can drink outside in public at this hour.

Milli's Bold Suggestion: Without missing a beat, Milli makes an unexpected suggestion. *"Then come to my place."* Nahar freezes for a moment, caught off guard. It's late at night, and her offer seems sudden, almost too bold. *"Are you sure?"* he asks hesitantly, unsure if it's a good idea given the time.

(Nahar's Surprise)

A mixed feeling, Nahar feels a rush of emotions-excitement, curiosity, and a bit of nervousness. It's not every day that Milli invites him over this late. He hesitates but doesn't want to seem unwilling. Her tone is casual, but there's an underlying tension that Nahar can't ignore.

A Decision to Make: As the clock ticks closer to midnight, Nahar's mind races. Should he accept the invitation? There's something thrilling about the idea, but the lateness of the hour and the surprise of her invitation leave him uncertain. "Okay, I'll come," he finally agrees, though his mind is still swirling with questions.

The Roommate's Advice

(Nahar's Dilemma)

Nahar's Uncertainty: As soon as Milli invites him over, Nahar feels a wave of hesitation. It's past midnight, and while he's intrigued, something about the situation feels off. Unsure of what to do, he decides to consult his roommate, Sumit, whose gut feelings have always been right.

Turning to Sumit: Nahar finds Sumit lying on his bed, headphones on. He explains the situation—the unexpected late-night invitation and his own uncertainty about going. *"Bro, I don't know if I should go. It's late, and this feels... strange."* Sumit listens calmly, his face thoughtful.

Sumit's Intuition

Sumit's Neutral Stance: Sumit, ever the rational one, shrugs and says, *"Look, it's your decision. I can't tell you what to do.*" But Nahar isn't satisfied with that answer. He knows Sumit's instincts have never steered him wrong before.

Pushing for an Answer: *"No, man, you always have a feeling about things. Tell me what you think,"* Nahar insists, almost pleading for guidance. Sumit sits up, looking more serious now. He takes a deep breath before replying.

The Turning Point

Sumit's Advice: After a pause, Sumit says, *"I don't know, Nahar. It's not about whether it's safe or not. The real question is, why now? Why did she invite you this late, all of a sudden? You know her better than anyone."* His words echo in Nahar's mind, and it becomes clear that even though Sumit isn't telling him outright not to go, there's a subtle warning hidden in his response.

Sumit leaves the choice up to Nahar, but his words weigh heavily on him. Nahar feels the pull to go, but also the lingering doubt that something isn't right.

(The Ride to Milli's Place)

As soon as Sumit gives the green light, Nahar feels a surge of excitement. He grabs the bottle, throws on his jacket, and checks his phone for Milli's location. In that moment, the thrill of doing something spontaneous makes his heart race. *"This is going to be fun,"* he thinks, trying to push aside the lingering doubts. Milli sends over the location. It's not too far, but it's in a part of town Nahar isn't overly familiar with. As he glances at the map, he feels a mix of anticipation and nerves. He quickly texts her, *"On my way."* Nahar grabs his bike keys and heads downstairs. The streets are quieter than usual, with only a few cars passing by. He revs the engine, feeling the cool night air against his face as he speeds off into the darkness. The thrill of the late-night ride and the thought of seeing Milli adds to his adrenaline.

As promised, just before he pulls out of the parking lot, Nahar shoots a text to Sumit. *"Heading to her place now, will text once I get there."* Sumit replies with a thumbs-up emoji, followed by, *"Be safe, bro."*

(Thoughts on the Way)

Nahar's mind races as he rides, his mind starts drifting back to their past conversations. The strange phone call where Milli said she didn't understand why they talked so much, the way she changed the topic afterward, and now this sudden invitation. It's all happening so fast. But Nahar shakes off the uneasy feelings, focusing instead on the excitement of the night ahead. As Nahar pulls up to Milli's place, the quietness of the night amplifies the sound of his bike engine cutting off. He parks the bike a little further away, trying to stay discreet, and makes his way to the front of the building.

His heart races, not from nerves this time, but from excitement as he approaches her door. To his surprise, Milli is already standing in front of the gate, a playful smile on her face. Her eyes light up when she sees him, and for a brief moment, all of Nahar's doubts seem to melt away. *"You made it!"* she says softly, clearly excited. Nahar walks up to her without a word, the bottle in hand, trying to contain his own grin. The air between them is charged with the thrill of secrecy. He reaches her doorstep, and for a moment, they just stand there, sharing a look that says more than words could. Milli steps aside, holding the door slightly ajar. *"Come on in, quietly,"* she whispers, her voice barely audible. Nahar steps in, his heart thudding in his chest, the adventure of the night pulling him deeper into the moment. And as Nahar reaches Milli's and enters her house, he pulls out his phone and sends a quick message to Sumit: *"Made it safely. All good here."* He smiles to himself, knowing Sumit will be waiting up for him, just in case. Milli watches, noticing his attention on the phone.

"Are you hungry? I was about to order some dinner," she asks casually, already scrolling through her phone for options. Nahar, still buzzing with excitement, shakes his head. *"I just had dinner with Sumit, so I'm good,"* he replies with a chuckle.

(The Comfortable Tension),

Milli shrugs and they both settle into the space, feeling a mix of comfort and the electricity of being together in such a secretive moment. Nahar glances around, noting down the simplicity of her room—a few books, some scattered belongings, and a sense of her personality everywhere. Nahar sets the bottle on the table between them, its presence symbolic of the night ahead. They exchange a brief smile before Milli turns and begins to prepare for their late-night drink, the air between them charged with anticipation.

(The Daredevil Vibe), Milli hands Nahar a glass of water, her eyes glancing over at the bottle resting on the table. There's a brief pause before she looks back at him, a playful grin spreading across her face. They both burst into laughter, the kind that comes from unspoken understanding. It's the laughter of two people who know they're about to cross a line—two daredevils about to defy the ordinary and embrace something reckless for the night.

(The Dare Set), As their laughter dies down, the energy between them shifts into something more adventurous. "Looks like we're really doing this," Milli says, her voice filled with excitement. Nahar nods, feeling the same surge of thrill as they, both get ready for what the night holds.

(Heading to the Terrace)

Gathering the Essentials without wasting any time, Milli moves swiftly. She grabs two glasses, some snacks from the kitchen, and a mat to sit on. Her energy is contagious, and Nahar can't help but admire how effortlessly she pulls it all together. He follows her, bottle in hand, as they make their way to the terrace.

The cool night breeze greets them as they step onto the terrace. The stars above seem brighter than usual, and the city below is quiet, adding to the feeling that they're in their own little world. Milli spreads out the mat, and they sit down, side by side, ready to start their night of adventure.

As they settle in, there's a quiet excitement in the air. Nahar uncorks the bottle, and for a moment, they both look at each other with that same playful grin they shared earlier. It feels like they're daring each other to take the first. Nahar uncorks the bottle and pours them both a drink. They clink their glasses together, and Milli takes the first sip. "To us," she says softly, her eyes glinting in the dim light of the terrace. Nahar nods, following suit with his own sip. The warmth of the drink contrasts with the cool night air. *"To us,"* he echoes, feeling a sense of calm settle over him as the alcohol slowly works its way into their system.

(Talking about Life)

As they sit on the mat, snacking on the ready-to-eat items, their conversation drifts from light topics to something deeper. Milli glances at the stars and says, "Do you ever think about what life will be like after all this? After the exams, the job search... the pressure?" There's a vulnerability in her voice that Nahar hasn't heard before.

He pauses before replying, "Yeah, I do. I think about it a lot, actually. Sometimes I wonder if all of this effort will be worth it. But then... I think about what we're trying to achieve and the dreams we've built, and it keeps me going." He looks at her, curious to hear her thoughts.

(Milli's Inner Conflict)

Milli sighs, taking another sip. *"I don't know... Sometimes I feel like I'm losing myself in all of this. Like, who am I, really, if I don't make it? What happens if I fail again?"* She doesn't look at Nahar as she speaks, staring out at the dark skyline instead.

Nahar reassuring her reaches out and touches her hand lightly, offering comfort. *"Hey, you're stronger than you think. You've already come so far, and whether you make it or not, it doesn't change who you are. You're Milli—determined, smart, and always pushing yourself."* His voice is steady, trying to soothe the uncertainty he senses in her.

(Vulnerability on Both Sides)

Milli turns to face him, her eyes searching his. *"You really believe that? I don't always feel like that person. Sometimes I feel like I'm faking it... like people expect me to be something, and I just go along with it."* Her voice trails off, and for a moment, there's silence between them.

Nahar takes a deep breath, feeling the honesty of the moment pulling him in. *"I get that. I feel it too. The pressure, the expectations... It's exhausting. But I guess we're all just trying to figure it out, one step at a time."* His words hang in the air as they both sit in the shared silence of their vulnerabilities.

(The Changing Dynamic)

As the night deepens, the bond between them feels more tangible. The conversation, mixed with the intimacy of the setting and the alcohol, creates a deeper connection taking them towards the Emotional Exchange. After a long pause, Milli rests her head on Nahar's shoulder. Her voice is softer now, almost a whisper. *"You know, sometimes I feel like I'm just pretending to be okay. That everything I've been working for is slipping away, and I don't even know who I am anymore."* The weight of her words lingers in the cool night air. Nahar feels her tension. He wraps his arm around her, trying to offer warmth and reassurance. *"You're not pretending, Milli. You're going through the same stuff we all are, trying to figure things out.*

But I know one thing for sure—you're stronger than you give yourself credit for."

Nahar's opening up to his own fears, feels a shift within himself too. For so long, he's held it together, pretending to be fine under the pressure of exams and their relationship. But tonight, something in Milli's vulnerability gives him the courage to open up. "I've been scared too, you know. Scared of failing, of not living up to everyone's expectations... even yours."

Milli lifts her head from his shoulder, her eyes searching his, "Mine?" she asks softly. "Why would you think that?"

"Because I didn't want to let you down. I wanted to be this guy who has it all figured out, but the truth is... I don't. And sometimes, I feel like I'm losing control, like I'm drowning in all these expectations." His voice cracks, and for the first time, Nahar shows a deeper vulnerability.

(The Shared Understanding)

Milli in solute empathy looks at him with understanding in her eyes. She gently reaches for his hand, holding it tight. *"We're both trying to be perfect, but we don't have to be, Nahar. I don't expect you to have all the answers. I just... I just want to be there for you, the way you're there for me."* Her words feel like a balm to the hidden fears they've both been carrying.

Nahar exhales deeply, feeling an immense relief he hadn't realized he needed. In that moment, it feels like they've peeled back a layer that had been keeping them apart, revealing something more real and raw. *"Maybe we're both just figuring it out as we go,"* he says quietly.

It's a calm, composed, moment of clarity and they sit in silence for a few moments, the weight of their confessions hanging between them. The night feels more intimate than ever, the stars above almost watching over them. For the first time, Nahar feels like they've reached a deeper understanding—not just as a couple, but as two individuals struggling with their own battles.

Milli finally breaks the silence. *"No matter what happens, Nahar, we'll face it together, right?"* Her voice is filled with quiet determination. Nahar squeezes her hand and nods, *"Together,"* he echoes.

(A calm after the storm)

After sharing their vulnerabilities, the air between them feels lighter. The weight of unspoken fears and insecurities has lifted, leaving behind a sense of calm. They sit side by side on the mat, quietly sipping their drinks, letting the silence speak for itself.

There's no need for words right now; the connection between them is enough. The alcohol warms their bodies, but the deeper warmth comes from the intimacy of the conversation they just had. Nahar feels a strange sense of peace, a quiet assurance that no matter how complicated life gets, this moment belongs only to them. Milli leans her head against his shoulder again, this time not out of fear or doubt, but because she feels safe. Nahar gazing up at the stars, his thoughts momentarily drifting. Without thinking, he points at a cluster of stars above them. *"See that? They call it Orion's Belt. My dad used to show me this when I was a kid."* His voice is soft, almost as if he's sharing a secret from a simpler time. Milli in curiosity now follows his gaze, a small smile forming on her lips. *"I've never really looked at the stars like that,"* she admits. *"They always seemed so far away, but right now... they don't seem that distant."* There's something poetic in her words, as if she's talking about more than just the stars.

(The Intimacy Deepens and the Physical Closeness both encounter) The conversation naturally slows, and they sit there, closer than ever before. Nahar can feel the warmth of Milli's body next to his, and it brings him a strange sense of comfort. The night air is cool, but it doesn't matter—they're wrapped in their own bubble of intimacy.

Milli suddenly chuckles, breaking the stillness. Nahar glances over at her, amused. *"What's so funny?"* he asks. She grins, a light-heartedness returning to her expression. *"I was just thinking about how we started this night. We were like two daredevils sneaking drinks on the terrace.*

Now look at us, talking about life under the stars. It's... kind of perfect". Nahar can't help but smile at her words. *"Yeah, it is perfect,"* he agrees. There's something about this moment that feels pure, as if the night has stripped away all the noise and left them with only what matters. Breathing the moment of playfulness as the heaviness of earlier fades, Milli nudges Nahar with her elbow. *"So, who's winning the next chess game?"* she asks with a mischievous glint in her eyes. Nahar chuckles, *"Oh, come on, you know I let you win last time."*

"Let me win? You're just making excuses because you don't want to admit I'm better," she teases. The playful banter is a welcome contrast to the earlier seriousness, and it feels like they've returned to the easy comfort of their friendship, but with a deeper bond now.

The night slowly fades and there's this peace of moment when they both grow calmingly quiet, the alcohol taking its toll and the emotional exhaustion is setting in. The city below seems to have fallen asleep, and the terrace feels like their own private world. Neither of them wants the night to end, but there's a mutual understanding that they've shared something special.

Nahar looks over at Milli one last time before the night winds down. *"I'm glad we had this talk,"* he says quietly. Milli nods, her eyes soft and full of affection. *"Me too. I think we needed it."* And with that, they sit in peaceful silence, their bond stronger than before. As their conversation winds down and the bottle empties, the terrace falls into a comfortable stillness. The cool night air wraps around them, but neither of them seems to notice. They've settled into a peaceful state, no longer needing words to communicate the closeness they now share. Milli, feeling the slight chill in the air, quietly grabs a single blanket they brought up earlier. Without saying a word, she drapes it over both of them. They lie side by side, staring up at the sky, the warmth of their bodies mingling under the cover. It's not awkward, just... natural. Both towards the nearness of sleep, exhausted from the emotional conversations feel the dizziness and the alcohol starts to catch up with them. Nahar feels his eyes growing heavy, but he doesn't want to break the moment. Milli seems to sense this too, as her head tilts slightly toward his. They lie in comfortable silence, listening to the soft sounds of the night around them.

(Close, But Not Too Close), Even though they're close, there's still a quiet restraint. Neither has moved closer deliberately, but as they both start to drift into sleep, the barriers between them seem to soften. The bond they've built, now unspoken, makes the closeness feel inevitable, yet pure.

As the first light of dawn begins to creep over the horizon, Nahar stirs slightly. His body feels the weight of something familiar but different. When he opens his eyes, he realizes just how close Milli is. Her face is inches from his, her breath warm against his skin. In this quiet moment, the world outside feels non-existent.

Nahar's heart races, not from fear or nerves, but from a newfound sense of intimacy. He can see Milli's chest rising and falling gently, still deep in sleep. The way she looks, peaceful and close to him, sends a warmth through him that's stronger than anything he's felt before.

Slowly, Milli stirs as well. Her eyes flutter open, and she realizes just how close they are. She doesn't pull away, nor does she seem surprised. Instead, her eyes meet Nahar's, and there's an unspoken understanding between them. It's as if, in that instant, they both know this was always going to happen. Milli offers a small, soft, sleepy smile. Nahar can't help but smile back. They don't speak—there's no need for words right now. The connection between them is palpable, and it fills the space with a warmth that neither of them wants to break.

(The First Kiss)

In the early morning light, without any hesitation or second thoughts, their faces slowly draw closer. The world around them fades as their lips meet softly for the first time. It's not rushed or filled with passion, but instead, it's tender, gentle, and filled with the emotions they've shared all night. The kiss lingers, slow and meaningful, as if they are both savouring the moment. This isn't just an act of desire—it's a reflection of the trust and susceptibility they've shared. Nahar's hand instinctively finds its way to Milli's, their fingers intertwining beneath the blanket as they share this quiet but profound moment. After a few seconds, they both pull back slightly, still holding each other's gaze. There's no need to explain what just happened. The kiss was the culmination of everything they've been building toward, a quiet affirmation that their bond had deepened in ways neither of them fully understood until now. There's no awkwardness, no uncertainty - only the peaceful realization that this was the right moment for them both. They continue lying there, still close, wrapped in the warmth of each other and the fading night.

(The Morning After) Awkwardness or Comfort?

When the sun rises to its complete, and reality settles in, both Nahar and Milli are unsure how to act. Should things feel different now? Should they talk about the kiss? Yet, despite these questions, there's a surprising calmness between them. They move slowly, packing up the blanket and glasses from the terrace, exchanging casual smiles. It's almost like the kiss was a natural progression rather than a disruptive event. As Nahar leaves her place, there's a brief moment where their eyes meet, both of them quietly acknowledging the night. There's no need to make any promises or commitments right away—yet there's an undeniable sense that their relationship has taken a significant step forward.

Chapter 14

The Cosy Kinship Amidst Conflicts

(An upsurge intimacy brings subtle changes in behaviour)

After the terrace night, the way Nahar and Milli interact changes ingenious. Their texts become a little more frequent, but there's more depth to the conversation. They now share small, intimate details of their lives they hadn't before, as if that kiss had unlocked a new level of trust.

Physical Closeness: When they meet, there's a natural shift in their body language. They sit closer, their arms brushing occasionally, their hands resting near each other, but they don't explicitly hold hands. It's as if the physical closeness is understood, not forced. Nahar finds himself instinctively protective of Milli, offering her his jacket when she's cold or holding open doors—small but noticeable acts of affection that weren't there before.

Even though they're growing closer, there's a lingering tension between them. The kiss, though meaningful, leaves unanswered questions: What are they now? Are they still friends, or has their relationship transformed into something more? Neither of them wants to address it just yet, fearful that putting it into words might change things too quickly.

(More Time Together), Nahar and Milli begin spending more time together, but now it's often just the two of them. The chess games continue, and so do their chai breaks, but the group study sessions with Adesh and Sudiksha become less frequent. Nahar feels an invisible pull to protect his time with Milli, yet he also starts feeling guilty about pushing his friends aside. This inner conflict starts to weigh on him. Nahar, Adesh, and Sudiksha are sitting at their usual study table in the library. The others are deep in their books, but Nahar's mind keeps drifting. He stares blankly at his notes, trying to focus but unable to shake off the emotional storm he's been going through with Milli.

(Sudiksha's Outburst), After watching Nahar struggle for a while, Sudiksha finally snaps. "Nahar! Where is your head these days? We're barely two months away from the exam, and you're acting like it's a year away. This is revision time, not dream time!" Her words cut through the fog in Nahar's mind, bringing him back to reality.

"Look," Sudiksha softens a little, realizing how hard she's coming down on him, "I know things are tough, but you've got to find a balance. You can't let this-whatever this is-ruin all the work you've put in. You've spent years preparing for this exam. Don't throw it all away because you're distracted. Manage both your life and your study time, or else…"

Nahar knows she's right, but managing his personal emotions alongside his study schedule seems overwhelming. Her words linger in his mind. He realizes he needs to recalibrate and refocus.

The news comes unexpectedly during a regular study session. Nahar, Ragini, Sudiksha, and Adesh are gathered in their usual spots, going through their notes when the administrator walks in and drops the bombshell: "Due to financial difficulties, the coaching centre and library will be closing next week". Nahar is the most affected, feeling the weight of the upcoming exam and now this new obstacle. The library had been his safe haven, a place where he could focus, away from the distractions of his personal life. His mind races—what will he do now? Where will the study? Initially in disbelief, she quickly shifts into problem-solving mode. "We need to find another place to study," she declares, already thinking of alternatives, but the frustration is evident in her voice. Ragini always optimistic, tries to keep the mood light, saying, "Maybe we can study at someone's home for a while. It won't be that bad." But even she knows how much of a setback this is. For Nahar, this closure feels like everything is falling apart at the worst possible time. Overwhelming stress, His emotional struggles with Milli, the pressure of his exams, and now losing the one place where he could focus—it all becomes too much. He knows that finding a new study space will be difficult, and it's another distraction he can't afford. Nahar's room now becomes the new hub for their study group. It's a small, modest room, with just enough space to accommodate everyone. The bookshelves are cluttered with notes and textbooks, and the bed is pushed aside to make space for the group to sit together. There's a sense of both urgency and desperation as they gather here, knowing the clock is ticking for their exams.

The transition feels strange at first. Nahar had always kept his room a personal space, but now it's filled with his friends every day. It becomes harder to keep his thoughts about Milli in check with her so close by, especially given the emotional complexities between them. There's a certain tension in the air, but the looming exams keep everyone focused—for now. With Sumit gone during the day, the group can study undisturbed. However, Nahar feels an odd emptiness when he leaves each morning, knowing that Sumit's usual intuition and support won't be there in the evenings when he needs to unwind from the day's work.

Chapter 15

Distant Catch-Up

The group is excited to be together again after intense weeks of study and exams. Laughter fills the air as they share stories of exam-day nerves, funny incidents, and plans for what's next. It's the first time they've all relaxed in a long time.

(Ruhi's return)

Ruhi's presence adds a nostalgic vibe. Since she had left for her job, her absence had been felt. Her return brings a burst of excitement as everyone catches her up on their lives. Her energy helps the group feel more complete again, and her perspective as someone working outside the study bubble gives fresh insight. Though Milli is not physically at the café, her presence lingers in Nahar's mind. Her support throughout his preparation makes Nahar feel quietly appreciative, even as he engages in conversations with his friends. He can't help but think back to her encouraging words before the exam. They both tease Nahar about his stress during the study period, but there's warmth in their jabs. They've all been there for one another, but they notice a change in Nahar-he's more centred, possibly because of Milli's influence.

Since Ruhi has been out of the study circle, she notices changes in everyone. And a drastic change she observes is in Nahar's behaviour. She is both surprised and shocked to watch Nahar's metamorphosis from so strong headed and disciplined boy into a completely changed one. Her heart aches to see how her close friend has undergone such a weird transformation. She asks Nahar more pointed questions, wanting to know about Milli and the bond they seem to share. There's a light heartedness in her tone, but her questions make Nahar feel a little exposed.

As Nahar returns to his room after the café reunion, there's a sense of anticipation in the air. He's waiting for Milli's call, knowing that their conversation might hold something different now that the exam phase is over. When the phone finally rings, Nahar answers with a mix of excitement and apprehension. She starts by asking about his exam experience, her tone warm and caring. Nahar explains how it went, but there's an unspoken layer beneath their words. Milli's voice carries a gentleness that comforts Nahar after the stressful day.

As they talk, the conversation flows naturally. They reminisce about the weeks of preparation, laugh about small moments they shared, and express relief that the pressure is finally behind them. The bond they've formed over this time feels strong, but Nahar still has lingering doubts that he tries to suppress. As the conversation bends down, Nahar mentions that he'll be leaving the city now that the exams are over. Milli falls silent for a moment, as though processing the news. This change represents a shift in their relationship's rhythm, and it's clear that Nahar's departure may alter things between them. Though Milli tries to be supportive, there's a noticeable shift in the mood after Nahar tells her he's leaving. Their conversation, once easy and flowing, becomes tinged with a quiet uncertainty. Will the distance affect their growing connection?

Chapter 16

The Erotic Spasm

In your eyes, I see the reflection of a love that knows no boundaries – pure, passionate, and eternal."

Both Nahar and Milli seem to be considering this, even if they don't say it out loud.

When Nahar arrives at Milli's place for what feels like a final meeting before he leaves for home, there's a quiet sense of urgency between them. It's been so long since they last saw each other, and the time apart has added layers to their emotions. As Milli offers chai, Nahar takes a deep breath, feeling the weight of everything they've gone through together.

Nahar looks at Milli, emotions swirling within him, and suddenly steps forward to embrace her tightly. The hug is more than just a physical act—it's his way of thanking her for being with him through the challenges, the long study hours, and the emotional rollercoaster they've both been on. He holds her like he doesn't want to let go, knowing that their future is uncertain.

Milli responds by wrapping her arms around him gently, but there's a subtle hesitation. It's as if she knows things are shifting, yet she doesn't pull away. In that moment, the hug speaks volumes, a mix of gratitude, affection, and perhaps even unspoken sadness. They've been through so much, and yet, here they are—on the verge of a new chapter. When they sit down with their chai, the atmosphere is heavy with unspoken words. There's warmth in their conversation, but also an undercurrent of tension. They talk about small things—the chai, the weather—but both know this could be one of their last private moments before Nahar leaves the city. As Nahar rests his head on Milli's thigh, the quiet of the moment speaks louder than words. The emotional connection between them deepens, and it's clear they're ready to take their relationship to the next level. In that peaceful silence, Milli leans down and gently kisses Nahar's lips, marking a turning point in their journey. This soft, intimate gesture seals their bond, and though no formal words are exchanged, they both understand that they've crossed into something more serious. As they move from the couch, their kisses grow deeper, and Nahar becomes increasingly aware of Milli's scent-a subtle fragrance that captivates him.

The scent lingers, drawing him closer with each moment. The soft light of the room casts a glow over them as they slowly make their way to the bedroom. Nahar gently but confidently guides her onto the bed, and they continue their passionate exchange. There's a sense of comfort and intensity that envelops them, as if their souls are intertwining with every touch, every kiss. The moment transcends the physical, making it feel like two spirits are merging, bound by more than just emotion. Their connection is palpable, as though they are finally expressing all that had been building up between them in this intimate, raw, and powerful moment. As the intensity between them builds, Nahar's lips trail down Milli's neck, and he gives her a gentle love bite, causing her to shiver with a mix of surprise and pleasure. Milli, in response, unbuttons Nahar's shirt with trembling fingers, her breathing quickening as the moment becomes more charged. Nahar's hands glide to her back, his touch slow and deliberate. His fingers move in delicate patterns over her skin, tracing her spine, sending waves of electricity through her body. With each subtle movement of his fingers, Milli's desire heightens, her body reacting instinctively to his touch. There's a palpable sense of lust and longing, as they both surrender to the passion that's been building between them for so long. In this intimate exchange, their connection reaches a new level, a physical manifestation of the emotional bond they share As they undress each other, their movements become increasingly urgent and filled with desire. Every touch sends waves of warmth through their bodies, and their heartbeats sync, pounding faster with every moment. Their skin brushes together as they become fully immersed in the moment, rolling on the bed, completely lost in one another. Each caress, each kiss, and every shared glance deepens their connection, intensifying the passion between them. Their bodies move in rhythm, every sensation heightened as they explore this new territory together. It feels as if time has slowed down, and nothing exists outside this intimate bubble they've created. Their breaths become ragged, their hands eager, and every moment is filled with the raw intensity of their emotions merging with the physical.

In this shared experience, Nahar and Milli reach a point of total vulnerability, where their passion for one another seems to envelop the room, making this moment more than just an act of physical connection—it's an expression of everything they've felt and everything they've been holding back. As her chest presses against his, their bodies become entwined in a deeper, more intense embrace.

Every kiss they share is slow, deliberate, and filled with passion. Nahar's hands explore her body, and as they drift lower, Milli's breath quickens. Her body reacts to his touch, a wave of pleasure surging through her. She moans softly, feeling the rising sensation of an orgasm. In response, she wraps her arms tightly around him, pulling him closer. Her leg moves between his, and they begin to rub against one another, their bodies naturally responding to the growing heat and desire between them. The closeness feels electric, the friction intensifying their shared pleasure. With every movement, their connection becomes more intimate, rawer, as they experience this overwhelming moment together. Their hearts race in unison, and it feels like the world has faded away, leaving only the sensation of their bodies intertwined, moving as one. The passion and pleasure they feel seem to merge, creating an overwhelming sense of release, as they lose themselves completely in each other. As the pleasure builds, Milli feels an intense sensation inside her, one that sends waves of ecstasy through her entire body. She can't control the rush of emotions, the overwhelming feeling of desire mixed with vulnerability, and it consumes her. Every touch, every movement amplifies the pleasure she feels, making her body tremble in response. Nahar, completely engrossed in the moment, notices the soft sheen of sweat forming on her face. A single drop of sweat trickles down her neck, accentuating the curve of her body, making her appear even more sensual in the dim light. The sight of her-lost in pleasure, flushed, and glowing-makes her even more irresistible to him.

That single drop, sliding slowly down her skin, seems to heighten the intensity of the moment. It symbolizes the rawness of their emotions, the purity of their desire, and the passion they've unleashed together. Their bodies move in sync, the pleasure building with every second, and in this intimate connection, they are both entirely vulnerable yet empowered by the intensity of their shared experience. As they both lie together, utterly spent, their bodies intertwined, they bask in the warmth and intimacy that surrounds them. The exhaustion from their passionate encounter slowly gives way to a gentle calm. Nahar, feeling the softness of Milli's body, tenderly wraps his arm around her, his fingers tracing the curves of her chest. With a quiet sigh, he leans his head against her breast, feeling her heartbeat against his cheek. Milli, still catching her breath, feels a deep sense of vulnerability and contentment. She remains still, her chest rising and falling with every deep breath she takes.

There's no need for words between them now; the silence speaks of trust and connection. As Nahar rests his face against her, she feels more open and exposed than ever before, yet entirely at peace with it. Her body is fully relaxed, and in this moment of closeness, she allows herself to embrace the intimacy, enjoying every sensation. The quietness of the room, their rhythmic breathing, and the closeness they share create a moment of serenity. Wrapped up in each other, they are lost in the sensation of their bodies touching—skin against skin, feeling connected in a way they never had before. It's a moment that transcends the physical, something more profound, as they simply exist together, enjoying the quiet after the storm of their passion. As they slowly regain their senses, both Nahar and Milli quietly reach for their scattered undergarments, slipping them back on without a word. The air between them is calm, the intensity of their earlier passion replaced by a soft, shared exhaustion. Nahar, his body still heavy with fatigue, notices the water bottle beside the bed. He grabs it, takes a long drink, and then turns to offer it to Milli. She accepts it with a small, tired smile, taking a few sips before placing it aside. Without speaking, they embrace once again, wrapping their arms around each other as they lie down on the bed. The world outside feels distant, unimportant, as they settle into the comfort of each other's warmth. Their bodies fit naturally, the exhaustion pulling them into a restful, contented stillness. The weight of what just transpired lingers in the room, but it feels peaceful, without any rush or expectation. For now, they are simply two people sharing a quiet moment, letting themselves drift into rest. The soft rhythm of their breathing eventually syncs, and in the comforting embrace of each other, they slowly surrender to sleep, feeling a sense of closeness that words could never fully capture. After a brief rest, Nahar and Milli wake up, both feeling the familiar pangs of hunger.

Milli decides to make rice, while Nahar quickly orders curry from a local restaurant. The afternoon is quiet as they prepare for their late lunch. Once everything is ready, they sit together at the small table in her room, enjoying the simple yet satisfying meal, exchanging a few smiles and soft laughter as they eat. As the sun begins to dip in the sky, casting a golden hue over the city, they move to the couch near the window. The sunset outside creates a serene, almost magical atmosphere. The soft colors of the sky—orange, pink, and lavender—bathe the room in a warm, gentle light. The air between them feels intimate yet peaceful, as if the entire world has slowed down just for them.

Sitting close together, they quietly watch the sun sink lower. Nahar, feeling the weight of the day's emotions and the deepening affection between them, gently rests his head on Milli's shoulder. She leans into him, her fingers lightly brushing his hand as they intertwine. The moment is quiet, yet full of meaning—a silent acknowledgment of their bond, stronger now than ever. The warmth of the setting sun, the soft breeze filtering through the window, and the closeness they share make the moment feel perfect, as if the universe has conspired to give them this peaceful, romantic evening. Neither of them speaks; there is no need to. In the simplicity of the moment, they are perfectly content, lost in the comfort of each other's company, their hearts in sync, as they watch the world turn golden around them. After the comfortable silence, Nahar finally breaks it, his voice low and serious. "I'm leaving tomorrow," he says softly, knowing the weight those words carry. Milli tenses beside him, her eyes filling with a sudden sadness. Without a word, she turns to face him, her expression emotional, and she pulls him into a tight hug, holding him close as if trying to stop time from moving forward. *"Isn't there any possibility for you to stay a little longer?"* she asks, her voice cracking slightly. Her arms around him tighten, as if she fears letting him go would make the inevitable feel even more real. Nahar sighs softly, feeling the conflict in his own heart, but he knows this moment had to come. *"I've already packed everything, and my ticket is confirmed. I can't change it,"* he explains, trying to sound reassuring. He strokes her back gently, feeling her heartbeat against his chest.

Milli looks up at him, her eyes searching his for some reassurance. Nahar cups her face, brushing away the strand of hair that has fallen over her tear-streaked cheek. "It doesn't matter how far apart we are," he says, his voice calm but full of affection. "We will always stay in touch, Milli. Nothing can change that. This isn't goodbye forever—it's just for now." She listens to his words, feeling comforted but still emotional. The weight of the moment begins to lift as she allows herself to believe him. "Okay," she whispers, wiping her eyes and nodding softly. "As long as we stay connected, I can manage". Nahar smiles, gently kissing her forehead. They sit in each other's embrace for a while longer, feeling the closeness between them, letting the reassurance of his words settle in. Despite the looming distance, the bond between them feels unbreakable. As the evening began to fade into twilight, Nahar leaned in to give Milli a soft goodbye kiss.

Their lips met gently, and it felt like time stood still, as if both were giving the impression of the last few moments they had together before Nahar's departure. Their eyes met in a shared understanding, full of unspoken emotions, as they both knew that parting was inevitable, but the connection they had built was unshakable. After the kiss, they turned to face the mirror near the window. Hand in hand, with Nahar's arm resting on Milli's shoulder, they looked at their reflection. For a moment, they simply stood there, absorbing the image of themselves together. It was bittersweet, seeing their love reflected back at them, knowing this moment would soon be a memory. Nahar broke the stillness by gently pulling Milli into one last, deep hug. He could feel her heartbeat against his chest, and he closed his eyes, trying to etch the feeling into his memory. Milli hugged him back tightly, her grip firm but full of tenderness, as though she didn't want to let go. When they finally pulled apart, there was a shared silence, neither wanting to say the final words. But Nahar knew he had to leave. He gave her one last look, filled with a mixture of love, gratitude, and sadness, before stepping out of the door, leaving behind all the memories they had created together in that space. As he walked down the street toward his room, the night air cool against his skin, Nahar carried with him the warmth of their moments, their laughter, and their kisses. Even though he was leaving the city, Milli was still with him—in his heart, his thoughts, and every memory they had shared. As Nahar entered his room for the last time, a wave of nostalgia washed over him. The walls seemed to echo with memories—the long study sessions, the late-night conversations, and the laughter shared with Sumit, his roommate whose wisdom and support had been a constant anchor. Nahar looked at Sumit's empty bed, recalling the countless moments of advice and friendship they had exchanged, always knowing Sumit had his back.

He sat on the edge of his bed, the quietness of the room almost suffocating in its stillness. His mind wandered to Ragini, Sudiksha, and Adesh, the friends who had seen him through every struggle, pushing him to grow, encouraging him to stay focused on his dream of passing the government exam. They were more than just friends; they were family. Nahar felt a tug of longing, knowing that this chapter of his life was closing. He glanced around the room, each corner holding a memory - whether it was the books stacked on the table, the cosy spot where they would all gather to study, or the playful arguments over who was going to order chai during late-night revisions.

In this quiet moment, the reality of leaving the room, his friends, and the routine he had become so accustomed to started to sink in. Yet, he also felt a sense of pride - he had grown so much, and the people around him had played a huge role in shaping the person he had become. As Nahar began to pack his remaining belongings, he couldn't help but smile, cherishing the friendships and memories he would carry with him as he embarked on the next chapter of his life. The next morning, as the sun barely rose, Nahar stood outside his room with his bags packed, ready to leave for home. His heart felt heavy, weighed down by the thought of leaving everything behind - his friends, the memories, and Milli. He tried to stay composed, but tears welled up in his eyes as Sumit walked him to the bus stop. Sumit, always the calm one, gave him a reassuring pat on the shoulder, their silent understanding stronger than words. As Nahar boarded the bus, he glanced back one last time at Sumit, who waved with a knowing smile. That smile carried all the support, care, and moments they had shared. Nahar took his seat by the window, plugging in his earphones and playing peaceful music to ease the whirlwind of emotions inside him. The bus engine roared to life, and it slowly started moving. As they passed the familiar streets, Nahar found himself silently retracing the paths of his memories. The coaching center, the library where it all began, the cafés where he and his friends had laughed after long study sessions—all flashed by like a reel of his life in the city. His heart ached with each landmark, knowing that this chapter was now over. The bus turned down a familiar road, and suddenly, Milli's building came into view. Nahar's breath caught in his chest as they passed by the very place where they had spent their final night together. He could almost feel her presence beside him, the warmth of their shared moments lingering in his heart. He touched the window lightly, as if reaching out for the memories, but the bus continued forward, leaving that part of his life behind. The city faded into the background as the bus picked up speed, and Nahar leaned back in his seat, closing his eyes. The music played softly in his ears, blending with the hum of the bus. A tear slid down his cheek, but he smiled through it, knowing that though he was leaving, the memories and the people he loved would stay with him, no matter how far he travelled.

Nahar's emotional depth and willingness to help others reflect his true strength, even though he appears weak at times. His vulnerability, especially in moments like leaving the city, reveals how much he cherishes connections with those close to him - like Milli, his friends, and even his memories of the places they've shared.

Chapter 17

Change in the Balance

Nahar's decision to stay home while continuing his exam preparation reflects his emotional resilience, despite the physical distance from his friends and Milli. His ability to adapt to these changes while maintaining connections shows how deeply rooted he is in both his relationships and his goals. The contrast between his emotional vulnerability and outward strength adds depth to his character, highlighting his unique ability to care for others while navigating his own challenges. As things progress smoothly between Nahar and Milli, their bond seems to strengthen through their regular late-night calls and messages. The consistency brings them closer, and after three to four months, Milli informs Nahar that there will be a change in her schedule, keeping her busy from morning to evening. Nahar, in his playful way, reassures her with a light -hearted comment, telling her not to forget to message him, subtly masking any potential concern he might have. This shift introduces a subtle change in their dynamic, and while Nahar jokes about it, it could hint at an underlying shift in their relationship as well. As time progressed, Nahar found himself noticing a change in Milli's behaviour, something that was hard to ignore. Their late-night calls and endless messages, which once flowed naturally, started to feel sporadic. Where they once shared moments effortlessly, Milli now seemed distant. Her responses became delayed, often filled with excuses about being busy or tired. Initially, Nahar brushed it off, convincing himself that she was simply overwhelmed with her own commitments. But as days turned into weeks, these changes in Milli's behaviour became too frequent to dismiss. Nahar started feeling the emotional disconnect. He could sense her drifting, and with that came an unsettling anxiety. Despite the love they shared, he couldn't help but wonder if something was wrong—something neither of them was talking about. There were small moments that should have brought them closer, but instead, they highlighted the gap between them. Milli would often miss Nahar's calls, and her replies to his messages would come after hours, sometimes with vague explanations like, "I was busy," or, "Sorry, I just saw this." Nahar's heart, which had always trusted her, now began filling with doubt. He knew her well enough to understand when something was off, but he didn't want to accept it. The emotional distance felt like a slow, creeping wave that neither of them seemed to know how to stop.

The more Nahar tried to reach out, the more distant Milli appeared. This growing frustration and tension finally came to a boiling point one day when Nahar, tired of the excuses and sensing her growing detachment, confronted Milli. His words, though not harsh, carried the weight of weeks of bottled-up emotions. He asked her why things had changed, why she was no longer the same person who used to share her every thought with him. Milli, perhaps sensing the pressure or just exhausted from juggling her own emotions, didn't respond the way Nahar expected. She became defensive, arguing that nothing had changed and that he was overthinking things. Nahar, deeply emotional and vulnerable, found himself caught in a spiral of confusion. This led to their first real fight—something that shook him because he'd always believed their bond was strong enough to withstand anything. As the fight escalated, Nahar's emotional side took over. He was someone who always gave more than he received, who helped others even when it cost him personally. This moment wasn't just about Milli's behaviour; it was about how Nahar, in his core, struggled with rejection and being misunderstood. The fight touched on his deepest fear—that the people he loved the most might leave him, just as Milli seemed to be doing. Despite feeling hurt and justified in his frustration, Nahar couldn't bear the thought of losing her. In the heat of the argument, he did something he'd done so many times before—he apologized. Even when he knew he wasn't wrong, even when the apology wasn't his to give, Nahar, with his emotional vulnerability, said, "I'm sorry." He apologized not because he believed he was at fault, but because peace with Milli meant more to him than being right. The apology settled the fight temporarily, and things seemed to return to normal, but deep inside, Nahar knew that the underlying issue hadn't gone away. He had smoothed over the surface, but the cracks in their relationship were still there, and he couldn't help but wonder when they might break wide open again. After a few days of reflection, Milli realized that the fault was hers. She had been distant, dismissive, and hadn't appreciated the efforts Nahar had made to hold their relationship together. It hit her hard when she thought about the fight, especially how Nahar had apologized despite being right, something she now saw as a sign of his love, not weakness. Guilt weighed heavily on her, and she knew she had hurt him deeply, even striking at his core—his self-respect. For Nahar, self-respect was everything. Throughout his life, he had prided himself on being someone who helped others and supported those in need, but never at the cost of his own values.

When he fought with Milli, it felt as though he had placed his self-respect at her feet, making himself vulnerable in a way that made him uncomfortable. He had apologized to her, but it left a lingering bitterness. The emotional strain had taken its toll, and in the days following their fight, Nahar found himself ignoring Milli's calls and messages. It wasn't out of malice, but a need to regain control of himself, to restore the dignity he felt he had compromised. Milli, sensing that she had crossed a line, began reaching out to him repeatedly. Her messages shifted from casual conversation to more earnest apologies. She admitted her mistakes and asked him to meet, hoping to make things right in person. At first, Nahar ignored her requests, his pride still bruised. He had given so much of himself to their relationship, and this recent episode felt like a betrayal of the trust they had built. How could he face her when he still felt like he had placed his self-worth second to their relationship?

Chapter 18

Rationalising the Behaviour

But after a few days of silence, the tension in Nahar began to soften. While his self-respect was vital to him, so too was the love he had for Milli. He had always believed in second chances, in the idea that people could grow from their mistakes. And deep down, Nahar knew that while Milli had hurt him, she was still the person who had stood by him in the past, who had shared both joyous and difficult moments with him. Eventually, after many requests from Milli, Nahar decided to admit to himself that perhaps this was an opportunity for them both to grow. He could forgive her, but it wouldn't be easy. He messaged her back, agreeing to meet. His reply was brief but clear: "I'll come to meet you." Though he wasn't sure how things would unfold, Nahar felt a sense of calm. He would approach this meeting with a heart that was both open and guarded, ready to see if they could rebuild what had been fractured. When they finally met, Nahar stood tall, his emotions more balanced than before. He knew this meeting wasn't just about Milli's apology; it was also about reclaiming the part of himself that had been hurt. This was a chance for him to express what he had been holding inside, to tell Milli that while love mattered, so did his self-respect. Nahar picked Milli up from her place early in the morning. The sun had just started to rise, casting a soft, golden glow over the city. They had decided to escape the usual surroundings and head to a peaceful lake in a nearby town, a place where they could be alone and talk without distractions. It felt like a fresh start, a chance to mend the cracks that had appeared in their relationship. As they reached the lake, the tranquillity of the place began to ease the tension that had lingered between them. The water was still, reflecting the sky like a mirror, and the soft chirping of birds added to the serene atmosphere. Nahar rented a pedalling boat, and they both climbed in, drifting slowly across the water. They were alone, with only the sound of the oars gently splashing in the lake as the boat glided further away from the shore. For a while, they remained silent, both of them taking in the calm surroundings. Then, as if gathering her courage, Milli turned to Nahar. She looked into his eyes, her voice soft but sincere, and admitted her mistake. She spoke about how she had ignored his efforts, and how deeply sorry she was for the hurt she had caused him. Nahar listened quietly, his expression calm. He had already forgiven her days ago, but hearing her speak so openly and vulnerably now was important to him.

It confirmed that she had reflected on her actions and understood the depth of what had happened. He smiled gently and told her, "I forgave you a long time ago. But it's good to hear you say all this. It means a lot."

With the weight of the apology off their shoulders, the atmosphere between them lightened. The boat drifted peacefully as they started talking again, this time with a sense of ease. Nahar made a joke, one of his usual light-hearted quips, and Milli burst out laughing. It was as if the tension melted away completely. They started cracking jokes, teasing each other, and laughing as the boat floated across the lake. Nahar and Milli were lost in each other's eyes, their conversation flowing smoothly. The connection they had felt before the recent fight seemed to return, stronger and more grounded. It wasn't just surface-level chatter; they were talking about everything, from their shared memories to their dreams and the future. Nahar felt more present than ever, as though this experience had deepened their bond. As their conversation deepened and laughter faded into a more intimate silence, Nahar and Milli found themselves instinctively reaching for each other's hands. The feeling was electric, just like the first time they had shared such a moment. There was an undeniable spark between them, one that seemed to reignite all the emotions they had been holding onto for so long. Milli, sensing the same current of emotions, gently took Nahar's hand and placed it on her thigh. He hesitated for a brief second, the sensation of her warmth beneath his touch filling him with a mix of excitement and nervousness. Slowly, he pressed her thigh, his touch becoming more assured as he felt her lean into him. Their eyes locked, and the world around them seemed to disappear. The calm lake, the distant sounds of nature, the soft glow of the morning sun—all of it faded as they inched closer to each other. Nahar could feel Milli's breath on his lips, their faces just inches apart, both ready to take the next step and kiss. But just as their lips were about to meet, Milli's phone rang, shattering the moment like glass. The sound was jarring in the quiet atmosphere, and they both froze, their rhythm broken. Milli quickly pulled back, fumbling for her phone while Nahar sat back, his heart still racing. There was an awkward pause, filled with the sudden intrusion of reality. Milli looked at the caller ID, hesitated, and then glanced at Nahar with a half-apologetic smile. The intimate bubble they had been in was gone, As Milli finished her call, she put her phone away, and both of them looked at each other, trying to shake off the sudden interruption.

Then, almost simultaneously, they burst into laughter. It was the kind of laughter that dissolved the awkwardness, a shared moment of understanding that lightened the mood. *"I guess the universe had other plans for us,"* Nahar joked, still grinning. *"Seems like it,"* Milli replied, playfully nudging him. Their conversation smoothly resumed, flowing naturally as they spoke about everything from their old memories to light-hearted teasing. The tension from earlier had completely evaporated, leaving them both feeling at ease. When the time on the boat came to an end, they paddled back to shore and stepped onto the dock. Nahar had prepared for the day by packing a simple but thoughtful lunch. They found a quiet table near the lake, the water reflecting the midday sun, creating a peaceful and picturesque scene.

Nahar unpacked the food, and they both sat down to eat, the gentle breeze making the moment even more serene. They shared their meal, talking about the little things—dreams, future plans, and how far they had come. Every now and then, they would look out at the lake, their conversation falling into comfortable silences, the kind that didn't need to be filled. Between bites, Milli leaned her head on Nahar's shoulder, sighing contentedly. "It's nice to just sit here with you like this," she said softly. Nahar smiled, feeling the same. "Yeah, it feels... simple, but perfect." As they sat by the lake, the peacefulness of the setting mirrored the calm that had returned between them. Whatever had come between them before now felt distant, washed away by the time they were sharing together. After their peaceful time by the lake, Milli had to rush off for her class. Nahar dropped her home, giving her a lingering hug before she hurried inside. They both parted reluctantly, knowing they had to get back to their responsibilities but secretly wishing they could spend more time together. As Nahar rode back home, his mind was filled with thoughts of Milli. Despite being focused on his studies, he couldn't shake the feeling of wanting to see her again. The moments they shared were always on his mind—her smile, her laughter, and the way they connected. He was obsessed with her presence, and the distance between their meetings only intensified the longing. Milli, too, felt the same. Between her classes and the increasing demands of her schedule, she found herself constantly thinking about Nahar. Every text, every call seemed like a lifeline, keeping them connected despite the physical distance. She was desperate to see him, just as he was to see her. Nahar immersed himself in his studies, knowing the importance of his preparation, but the moments of silence were always filled with thoughts of Milli. He'd often pause, wondering what she was doing, tempted to text her, even though he knew she'd be busy with her classes. It was like an unspoken pull, where they both knew they needed to stay focused, yet their minds couldn't help but wander back to each other. Each day felt like a waiting game—counting down until the next time they could meet, touch, and share another moment together.

Chapter 19

Regaining Composure

Their connection had grown so deep that being apart, even for a short time, felt unbearable. After a few months of everything going smoothly, Milli's health started to decline. Nahar noticed from their conversations that something wasn't quite right. She sounded tired and distant, and when he asked, she admitted she hadn't been feeling well for about a week. Concerned, Nahar couldn't wait any longer and decided to visit her in her city. When he arrived at her place, Milli's face lit up the moment she saw him. Despite her illness, his presence seemed to lift her spirits. Nahar brought some fruits, hoping to help her feel a little better. He walked into her room, and though she smiled, he could see the exhaustion in her eyes. She was clearly battling something that had drained her energy. Milli tried to stay cheerful for Nahar's sake, but her illness had taken its toll. As they sat together, Nahar could sense her strength was fading. He reached out and took her hand, squeezing it gently as a way of showing support. She smiled weakly, grateful that he was there with her. Even though Milli was trying to stay positive, there was a sadness in her eyes. Nahar could tell she was feeling vulnerable, perhaps frustrated with her own body for not keeping up with her normally vibrant spirit. He leaned in, brushing a strand of hair away from her face, and quietly reassured her, telling her to take her time and focus on getting better. Milli asked Nahar to stay with her for the day, not wanting to be alone while she wasn't feeling well. Without hesitation, Nahar agreed, understanding how much she needed him in that moment. They decided to make dinner together, a quiet, intimate activity that allowed them to focus on something simple amidst the heaviness of her illness. Though Nahar wasn't the best cook, he did his best to help Milli, following her instructions and doing whatever he could. He chopped vegetables clumsily, making her laugh at his attempts, and tried to stir the pot without spilling. Despite the buoyancy, there was a tenderness in the air as they worked side by side, creating a small moment of normalcy in a difficult time. As the meal came together, Nahar took on the role of serving the food, plating it carefully and making sure Milli had everything she needed. They sat down to eat, the warm smell of their simple homemade dinner filling the room. Nahar watched Milli closely, still concerned about her health, but she reassured him with a gentle smile.

While they ate, Nahar spoke softly, telling her to take good care of herself, to rest and not push herself too hard. His words were filled with genuine care, his love for her evident in the way he wanted her to be well again. Milli, touched by his concern, promised she would try to take better care of herself, though she couldn't help but tease him about his cooking skills.

They spent the rest of the evening quietly enjoying each other's company. Even though the situation wasn't perfect, Nahar's presence made everything a little better for Milli. As they sat together, the bond between them felt unshakable, and the love they shared deepened, solidified by this moment of vulnerability. As Nahar and Milli sat on the couch, the atmosphere was wrapped in a calmness that felt almost otherworldly. Outside, the stars flickered gently against the vast canvas of the night, casting a soft glow through the window. The coldness in the air only heightened the feeling of intimacy between them. Milli, looking somewhat fragile due to her recent illness, gently snuggled into Nahar's side, seeking both physical warmth and emotional comfort. Nahar could feel the weight of her head resting on his shoulder, her breath steady but quieter than usual. Nahar, ever aware of Milli's condition, wrapped his arm around her, pulling her in just a little closer, as if to shield her from everything that had been weighing her down. The room was dimly lit, the only real light coming from the faint glimmer of stars outside and the occasional gleam of streetlights in the distance. It was one of those rare moments where words seemed unnecessary. Their connection, their shared history, and the emotions they had both been through recently hung in the air, unspoken but palpable. They exchanged a few words here and there, mostly about how Milli had been feeling and what the coming weeks might look like for both of them. Nahar reassured her that everything would be alright, urging her to rest more and take better care of herself. Milli responded softly, her voice low but filled with gratitude, not just for his words but for his presence. Even in her weakened state, she managed to make him smile with small jokes, teasing him about how terrible his cooking had been earlier when he'd tried to help with dinner. The silence between them was peaceful, not awkward or heavy. It was the kind of silence that only two people deeply connected can share, where words aren't needed to fill the space because the feeling of being together is enough. Nahar's fingers gently traced the curve of Milli's arm, a quiet gesture that spoke volumes about how much he cared. She, in turn, nestled deeper into him, feeling the steady beat of his heart against her cheek.

Occasionally, they would both look out the window at the stars. The cold night seemed to stretch endlessly, but in that small room, they created their own little world. The outside faded away as their focus remained on each other. Nahar could feel the weight of everything that had happened recently—the distance between them during their studies, the small misunderstandings, the emotional roller coaster they'd been on—melt away in this moment of quiet connection. Every so often, Milli would look up at Nahar, and they would share a glance that spoke of affection, gratitude, and a kind of unspoken promise. Her illness had made her more vulnerable, and Nahar's presence was a source of stability for her. She closed her eyes at times, not to sleep but to savor the warmth of being held by someone who truly cared.

As the night grew colder, Nahar subtly adjusted the blanket around them, making sure Milli was comfortable. There was an unspoken understanding that this night, this moment, was theirs—a small oasis of calm amidst the chaos of life. Even though words were few, every touch, every glance, and every breath they took seemed to bring them closer. At one point, Milli gently placed her hand on Nahar's chest, feeling the steady rhythm of his heart. It was a quiet gesture, one that spoke of trust and affection. Nahar, sensing her need for closeness, tilted his head slightly to rest against hers. The world outside may have been cold, but between them, there was warmth, connection, and love. Eventually, the conversation dwindled into silence, but it wasn't an uncomfortable one. They sat like that for what felt like hours, neither needing to break the peaceful stillness. The night passed slowly, but neither of them minded. They were content in each other's presence, enjoying the quiet and the sense of being truly understood. Even with Milli's illness casting a shadow over things, for that night, they had each other, and that was enough. As they sat together, the world outside felt distant, almost irrelevant. The only thing that mattered was the comfort they found in each other's presence—the warmth that came from simply being together. And in that moment, they both knew that no matter what challenges lay ahead, they would face them, knowing that they could always find peace in each other. As Nahar noticed Milli's eyes slowly closing, her exhaustion evident from both the illness and the calm of the night, he gently whispered, "You should get some rest, Milli. Come on, let's go to bed." His voice was soft, filled with care and tenderness, not wanting to disturb the peace they had built. Milli, without much resistance, nodded lightly, her tiredness settling in.

He helped her up from the couch, their fingers still loosely intertwined as they walked together to the bedroom. The room was quiet, filled only with the faint sound of the cold breeze outside, and the bed seemed inviting after the long day. Nahar pulled back the blanket for her, allowing Milli to settle in first. She curled up comfortably, watching him as he climbed in next to her. Without a word, they found themselves naturally gravitating toward each other. Nahar wrapped his arms around her, pulling her close as they lay side by side. Milli's head rested gently on his chest, listening to the soft rhythm of his heartbeat. The warmth between them was undeniable, a sense of comfort and security that made the room feel even cosier. Nahar gently stroked her hair, feeling the softness between his fingers as Milli closed her eyes completely, letting go of all the weight she had been carrying. It was as though the world outside no longer existed, and in that moment, all that mattered was being in each other's arms. He could feel her breathing slow down as she drifted into a peaceful sleep. He kissed the top of her head softly, his lips brushing against her hair as he whispered, "Goodnight, Milli." Holding her close, Nahar felt a deep sense of contentment wash over him. It had been a long day, filled with emotion, but here they were, together, safe in each other's embrace. As they lay there, hugged tightly under the blankets, Nahar too began to feel the pull of sleep, the warmth of Milli against him acting like a lullaby. And soon, with her in his arms, they both drifted off into a restful sleep, wrapped in each other's comfort and love. In the middle of the night, Nahar woke up feeling a bit thirsty. Carefully, he untangled himself from Milli's arms, trying not to disturb her, and quietly reached for the water bottle on the bedside table. As he took a sip, the sound of the bottle cap twisting open stirred Milli from her sleep. She blinked a few times, still groggy, and turned to Nahar. "Do you want something to eat?" she asked softly, her voice barely above a whisper, filled with concern and care. Nahar smiled warmly at her, shaking his head. "No, I'm good, just needed some water," he reassured her, his voice low and comforting. He placed the bottle back on the table and gently settled back into bed beside her. As he pulled the blanket over both of them again, Milli turned to face him, her eyes soft but full of emotion. "Thank you, Nahar," she whispered, her voice sincere. "For everything today... for coming here and taking care of me." Nahar, feeling the warmth of her gratitude, gently brushed a strand of hair away from her face and smiled. "You don't need to thank me, Milli. I'm just happy to be here with you". Milli's expression softened even more, and she reached out to hold his hand. "It means a lot, though.

You always make things better," she said, her eyes reflecting the love and appreciation she felt for him. They shared a quiet moment, gazing into each other's eyes, the connection between them growing stronger. Nahar squeezed her hand gently. "Get some rest, Milli. You need to take care of yourself". With that, they both nestled back under the blanket, this time with an even deeper sense of closeness. As they lay in the quiet darkness, with only the soft hum of the night around them, Milli broke the silence with a question that had been lingering between them for some time. "Nahar... what is this between us?" she asked softly, her voice almost trembling. She turned slightly, her face close to his, her eyes searching for something in his expression. Nahar's heart skipped a beat. He knew what she was asking, but the words still caught him off guard. He wasn't ready for this conversation, not now, not when things felt so peaceful. He looked at her, trying to buy a moment to think, but her gaze was so earnest, so full of hope and curiosity, that he couldn't escape it. "You never said anything," Milli continued, her voice gentle but with a hint of vulnerability. "You never... proposed or gave this a name." She looked down for a moment, playing with the edge of the blanket. "Do you ever think about us like that? Or am I just..." Her voice trailed off, unsure of how to finish. Nahar felt his chest tighten. He had thought about it, many times. But putting a name to what they had—it felt like it would change everything. They had this beautiful, natural bond that didn't need labels, and yet, he knew how important it was for her to hear something more. "I..." Nahar started, feeling the weight of her question. "Milli, you know how much you mean to me," he said, his voice soft but sincere. "I just—" He paused, struggling with how to explain the complexity of his feelings. "It's not that I don't think about us or what we have... I just didn't want to rush things or change what's already perfect between us." Milli listened quietly, her eyes searching his face for more. She wasn't convinced. "But you never say it, Nahar. You never tell me what's in your heart. I... I need to know. Are we just... this? Or is there more?" Nahar felt the weight of her words pressing on him. He wasn't sure how to respond. He cared deeply for Milli—he loved her, in fact—but saying it out loud, giving it a name, felt like stepping into a new territory, one he wasn't sure he was ready for. "I don't want to lose what we have," he said, his voice barely above a whisper. "What if naming it changes everything? I'm scared, Milli." His honesty took him by surprise, but he couldn't hide it from her anymore.

Milli's expression softened, and she reached out to touch his face. "I'm scared too, Nahar," she admitted, her eyes glistening with emotion. "But I need to know what this is for us. It's not just about a name... it's about knowing we're on the same page, that we're in this together." Nahar took a deep breath, trying to gather his thoughts. He didn't want to leave her hanging or uncertain. "Milli... I love you. I've always loved you. I just didn't know how to say it," he finally confessed, the words spilling out with a mix of relief and fear. Her eyes widened, and a smile broke across her face, though there were tears forming in her eyes. "That's all I needed to hear," she whispered, her voice trembling. She leaned in and kissed him softly, a kiss full of love and understanding. In that moment, the tension between them melted away. Though Nahar hadn't fully answered every question she had, the confession of his feelings brought them closer than ever before. They held each other tighter, knowing that no matter what the future held, they were in this together. In that moment, everything felt right. Nahar leaned in and kissed her softly, their lips meeting with a newfound sense of security and love. It wasn't just a kiss— it was the beginning of something more, a commitment to each other that they had both been yearning for. They had finally given a name to what they had, and it filled them both with a deep sense of peace. After their heartfelt exchange, they cuddled close, their bodies entwined under the covers. There was no more uncertainty, no more hesitation. They were together in every sense now, and that thought brought them comfort. Softly, Nahar held her in his arms, feeling her breath steady as they lay in the quiet of the night. They both smiled, content and satisfied with the new chapter they had just opened in their lives. Slowly, they drifted off to sleep, still wrapped in each other's arms, their love now stronger than ever. The next morning, sunlight streamed gently through the curtains, casting a warm glow across the room. Nahar stirred first, knowing that it was time to leave, though part of him wished he could stay longer. As he quietly got up, Milli opened her eyes and smiled softly at him, still sleepy but aware of what the morning held. Without needing to say much, Milli got up and went to iron his shirt, making sure everything was just right. As Nahar watched her, he felt a sense of bittersweet gratitude.

This was what he had always wanted—a love filled with warmth and simplicity. The air between them was filled with unspoken emotions, both happy and melancholic at the thought of parting. Once his shirt was perfectly pressed, they sat down together for a cup of tea. The conversation was light, but their connection ran deep. They both knew the moment of goodbye was coming, but they cherished these last moments together. After the tea, Nahar stood by the door, and before leaving, he turned to Milli. He gently cupped her face in his hands and kissed her forehead, then her lips, lingering for a moment. She wrapped her arms around him in a warm embrace, neither wanting to let go. "Take care of yourself, Milli," Nahar whispered into her ear. "I'll miss you."

"I'll miss you too," she replied softly, her voice tinged with emotion. "Come back soon."

With one last warm hug, Nahar reluctantly pulled away. He glanced back at her one final time as he stepped out, the city already starting to bustle with the morning activity. As he walked away, his heart felt heavy yet full, carrying with him the memories of their time together. The city that had once been a place of studies, friendships, and love was now a chapter behind him. And with that, Nahar left the city, knowing that their bond had only grown stronger, even as the distance between them widened.

Chapter 20

Newfound Intimacy

After Nahar returns from visiting Milli, their bond seems to strengthen more than ever before. The physical closeness they shared at her place lingers in their minds, leaving them emotionally charged and deeply connected. They find themselves wanting to talk more, share more, and be part of each other's lives even more intensely. Nahar and Milli settle into a routine where they exchange messages throughout the day. Nahar would text her the moment he wakes up, asking about her health or simply saying good morning, and Milli would respond with a voice note of her morning routine. They have started sharing even the most mundane details of their day, such as what they ate for lunch or how the weather is. Every night, their calls last for hours. Milli talks about her classes, and Nahar shares how his studies are progressing. They joke, tease, and sometimes just sit in silence, comfortable in each other's presence, even if it's just over the phone. The future becomes a frequent topic. They begin to wonder aloud what it would be like to live together one day or how they would celebrate when Nahar finishes his exams or when Milli completes her course. They dream of vacations they'll take and future weekends spent together, far from the stresses of their separate lives. They might imagine renting a small apartment in a quiet neighbourhood, discussing the type of furniture they'd like, and making plans for weekend road trips.

(Emotional Intimacy and Dependence)

Their emotional connection deepens, but along with it comes an unspoken emotional dependence. Nahar, always the more sensitive one, starts to rely on Milli for emotional support. After long, stressful study sessions, he looks forward to hearing her voice, which calms him. Similarly, Milli, recovering from her health issues, starts depending on Nahar for reassurance and support. Nahar might begin calling Milli as soon as he feels overwhelmed with his studies, even if she's busy. Similarly, Milli, feeling insecure about her recovery, might call Nahar frequently, seeking comfort in his words.

(Emotional Validation): Nahar begins to feel that he needs Milli's approval for many things, whether it's a choice about his studies or personal decisions. He has always been emotionally vulnerable, and now, her opinions start to weigh heavily on him. He doesn't

realize it, but he's becoming emotionally reliant on her to feel secure. If Milli praises Nahar for his efforts in his studies, he feels great; if she's preoccupied and doesn't respond with enthusiasm, he starts questioning himself. On the other side, Milli, despite being more pragmatic, also becomes anxious when Nahar isn't immediately available. She begins to expect his constant attention and feels uneasy when his replies take longer than usual. This growing anxiety begins to manifest in subtle ways, like sending multiple messages when Nahar doesn't respond promptly. If Nahar is late in replying, Milli might send him multiple texts like, "Everything okay?" or "Are you busy?" These subtle messages point toward her increasing need for reassurance.

(Unrealistic Expectations and the pressure to Maintain Closeness)

As they grow closer, the pressure to maintain this level of emotional and physical closeness intensifies. Nahar, who values Milli's affection and attention, starts feeling like he must be the perfect boyfriend. He doesn't want to disappoint her, so he often goes out of his way to be available, even if it's at the cost of his own personal time or studies.

Nahar might cancel study plans just to stay on the phone with Milli or avoid spending time with his friends because he feels guilty if Milli's free and waiting for him.

Milli, on the other hand, starts feeling like she needs to be more for Nahar. She feels guilty about her health and not being able to give Nahar all the attention he deserves. This guilt leads her to overcompensate by being overly accommodating, which adds to the emotional strain on their relationship. Even when Milli feels tired or sick, she pushes herself to stay up late on calls with Nahar, afraid that he might feel neglected if she doesn't give him enough time. Both Nahar and Milli are walking on a tightrope, afraid of disrupting the delicate balance they've created. Though they haven't openly addressed it, the growing emotional dependence and heightened expectations begin to weigh them down. Neither wants to acknowledge that the relationship is starting to feel a bit overwhelming. If they go a day without talking much, both of them start feeling uneasy. Nahar might start wondering if something's wrong, while Milli might feel guilty about not making enough effort.

(Subtle Signs of Strain), Despite their strong emotional bond, small cracks begin to show. Nahar starts to feel guilty for relying so much on Milli, especially since he knows she's still recovering from her health issues. He becomes more self-conscious about how often he reaches out to her and starts pulling back slightly, afraid that he might be burdening her. Nahar might start replying with shorter texts or avoiding deeper conversations, convincing himself that he's just giving Milli space, even though he's worried about distancing himself.

On the other hand, Milli, now feeling the weight of Nahar's emotional needs, starts withdrawing ever so slightly. She still loves him deeply, but the emotional intensity of their relationship is beginning to overwhelm her. She's afraid of disappointing him but also realizes that they both need space. She begins to respond later than usual or becomes preoccupied during calls. During one of their nightly calls, Milli might sound distracted, mentioning that she's exhausted from the day. Nahar might notice but doesn't confront it, fearing that bringing it up would cause unnecessary tension.

Chapter 21

Brewing Conflict

As the days go by, Nahar starts doubting himself. He senses Milli's slight withdrawal but brushes it off, telling himself it's just temporary. However, it starts to affect his confidence, making him question whether he's doing enough or if something is wrong with their relationship. He might start overthinking Milli's delayed replies or second-guessing every word he says to her, worrying that he's pushing her away. Milli, too, feels conflicted. She knows she still cares deeply for Nahar, but the constant emotional back-and-forth is exhausting. She's unsure how to communicate this to Nahar without hurting him, so she keeps it bottled up, which only makes things worse. Milli might find herself wanting to talk less, simply because she needs some emotional space, but she hesitates to say anything, fearing it will cause a fight.

(A Build-Up of Frustration), Over time, the emotional strain begins to take its toll. Nahar, feeling increasingly insecure, starts questioning Milli's commitment, even

though she hasn't done anything overtly wrong. Milli, on the other hand, starts feeling suffocated, not because of Nahar's actions but because of the emotional intensity of their relationship. One evening, Nahar might ask Milli why she's been replying late or sounding distant on the phone. Milli, caught off guard, might get defensive, saying she's just tired or overwhelmed. This conversation could be the beginning of a larger rift. As they both grapple with their emotions, they might end up in a situation where they feel like they're walking on eggshells around each other, afraid to say the wrong thing. The relationship, once full of light and warmth, starts feeling heavy, weighed down by emotional dependence and unspoken expectations. Nahar might try to apologize, even if he's not sure what he's apologizing for, while Milli might reassure him but feel drained by the constant need to explain herself. Both are left feeling uneasy but unsure how to fix things. This more complex and emotionally charged version of Nahar and Milli's relationship sets the stage for future conflicts and challenges. They love each other deeply, but the pressures of emotional dependence and unspoken expectations make their relationship fragile. As they continue to navigate the complexities of love, they must also find ways to communicate openly and balance their needs with their own individual growth.

After Nahar and Milli's relationship becomes closer than ever, things begin to settle into a comfortable routine. They talk regularly, share their daily schedules, and enjoy frequent phone calls and late-night conversations. For a few months, everything feels like it's back to normal, even better than before. However, over time, Nahar begins to notice a shift in Milli's behaviour once again. Milli starts to distance herself, responding late to texts and becoming less engaged in their conversations. Her excuses for being busy become more frequent, and Nahar feels the same emotional disconnect that had troubled their relationship before. Despite his efforts to keep things smooth, the pattern is clear to him: Milli is withdrawing, and their bond is weakening. As this behaviour continues, Nahar comes to the realization that Milli is not suited for a long-distance relationship. He recognizes that she struggles to maintain the emotional investment necessary to keep them connected while they are apart. This understanding leaves him feeling disappointed but also more aware of their differences. Though they share a strong bond, their ability to manage a long-distance relationship is fundamentally incompatible. Nahar tries to confront Milli about her behaviour but she is evasive, offering vague explanations for her actions. She admits to being busy but doesn't fully address the emotional distance she is creating. Over time, Nahar realizes that it's not just a temporary phase—Milli is genuinely unable to provide the level of emotional connection he needs. He begins to pull back as well, emotionally preparing himself for what seems like an inevitable end. The relationship continues to unravel slowly. While they still care for each other, both Nahar and Milli understand that the effort to sustain their relationship is waning. Nahar stops reaching out as frequently, and Milli doesn't push to keep things going. Their bond fades gradually without a formal breakup, as both accept that they are drifting apart. It's a quiet dissolution, not marked by any dramatic ending, but by the mutual recognition that their relationship has run its course. In the end, they move on, carrying the memories of their time together, but understanding that they were not meant to last in the long term. Their emotional and physical distance proves too great, and while their love was real, it wasn't enough to sustain the relationship. Nahar's growing awareness of Milli's behaviour leads him to a deeper realization about her character. Over time, he notices a troubling pattern: Milli doesn't seem to hesitate when it comes to shifting her attention to someone else.

It becomes increasingly clear to Nahar that if he's not physically present in her life, she has no qualms about moving on to someone else for companionship or emotional support. This realization weighs heavily on him, as it conflicts with the deep emotional connection he thought they shared. Nahar begins to see that Milli is someone who struggles with loyalty when distance or time comes between them. He recalls moments when her interest in him seemed to wane without any major issues in their relationship—simply because he wasn't around as much. It feels like Milli's affection is tied to who is present at the moment, and Nahar starts questioning whether she truly values their bond or if she is just seeking the comfort of whoever is close by. This understanding makes Nahar feel both disappointed and wary. He realizes that Milli doesn't take time to reflect or resolve her feelings when things get difficult. Instead, she switches her attention to another person as if it's the easiest option, without considering the emotional consequences. Nahar, who values commitment and deep emotional bonds, finds it hard to reconcile with Milli's apparent ease in moving on from one person to another. As much as Nahar loves Milli, this revelation shifts his perspective on their relationship. He sees now that Milli isn't capable of giving him the security and loyalty he needs. Her tendency to drift toward others when things aren't perfect shows a lack of emotional maturity and commitment. This awareness makes him guarded, knowing that any time he's not physically there, Milli could be finding comfort in someone else's presence. This realization marks a turning point for Nahar. While he still cares for Milli, he begins to detach emotionally, knowing that their relationship is fragile and dependent on circumstances rather than true devotion. He starts preparing himself for the inevitable—understanding that Milli might not be the kind of person who can sustain a deep, lasting relationship without constantly seeking something new. It becomes clear to Nahar that this pattern will continue unless he takes control of his own emotional well-being, choosing to prioritize his self-respect over a relationship that no longer feels secure. Nahar is caught in an emotional turmoil that he can't escape. Despite everything he's observed about Milli—her seeming disinterest, her tendency to drift away when things aren't perfect—he's still deeply in love with her. He knows, in his heart, that his feelings for her run too deep to simply walk away. Nahar can't ignore the emotional connection they once shared, the memories they've built, and the bond that meant everything to him. It's as if every part of his being is tethered to her, even though he knows something has shifted.

For Nahar, relationships carry immense weight. He believes in loyalty, depth, and shared growth, and these values anchor him in his bond with Milli. Losing her isn't just about ending a relationship—it feels like losing a piece of himself. The thought of letting go is terrifying, not only because he still loves her, but also because he has invested so much emotionally. It's not easy for him to discard everything they've built together, even though he knows something is off. At the same time, Nahar feels the painful disconnect between his unwavering commitment and Milli's apparent indifference. While the relationship still holds meaning for him, it seems to have lost its spark for her. Nahar senses that she's growing bored with the routine and is no longer invested in the relationship the way he is. The late-night conversations, the inside jokes, and the shared dreams that once brought them closer now seem to be fading, leaving Nahar struggling to reignite a flame that Milli might not want to tend to anymore. Despite these feelings, Nahar is paralyzed by his love for her. He doesn't want to lose her, no matter how much the situation hurts. He keeps hoping that things will change, that she will realize what they have and come back to him with the same passion and commitment they once shared. He tries to justify her behaviour, convincing himself that it's just a phase or a rough patch they need to work through. But the truth is inescapable—Nahar knows deep down that the relationship isn't equal anymore. For him, the bond they share is everything, but for Milli, it feels like just another part of her life, one that she can drift away from when it no longer excites her. This imbalance is emotionally exhausting for Nahar. He feels like he's constantly the one pulling the weight of the relationship, making the effort to keep things alive, while Milli seems content to let things fizzle out without a fight. Yet, Nahar doesn't know how to let go. His heart still clings to the hope that she will come back fully, that she will see how much he cares, and that their relationship will once again hold the importance for her that it does for him. But the fear of losing her and the pain of her growing disinterest create an emotional limbo that Nahar can't escape from. He's stuck between wanting to hold on and realizing that maybe, no matter how much he tries, he's already lost her. Nahar finds himself caught in a dilemma—his love for Milli is unquestionable, but it's becoming increasingly clear that what Milli wants from their relationship is something he cannot consistently provide.

For Milli, Nahar's physical presence is essential. She craves the comfort of having him nearby, the daily proximity that reassures her and grounds the relationship. She thrives on the tangible connection—touch, shared space, and spontaneous moments. This emotional need for closeness creates tension as Nahar realizes that his absence causes her to feel distant, and ultimately, disconnected. For Nahar, it's a painful realization. His life, career ambitions, and personal responsibilities don't allow him to be physically present all the time. His long-distance commitment to Milli is genuine, but his absence is unavoidable. He has his goals and aspirations—things he can't sacrifice, even for love. Though he treasures their relationship, he also understands that life sometimes requires distance, and he's willing to make it work through communication, trust, and emotional intimacy. Milli, however, is someone who struggles with the idea of a long-distance relationship. While she might care for Nahar, she's emotionally driven by his presence. Without it, she feels a void that leaves her vulnerable to loneliness, a feeling that pushes her to seek comfort elsewhere, consciously or unconsciously. Her behaviour, whether intentional or not, suggests that when Nahar isn't physically around, she begins to drift. She craves companionship that goes beyond phone calls or messages; she needs someone physically present to fill that emotional space. This dynamic is tearing them apart. For Nahar, it's an unbearable burden. He understands that he can't be everywhere at once, and no matter how much he loves her, he can't satisfy her need for constant physical presence. His absence isn't a sign of emotional neglect; rather, it's part of the reality of his life. He's invested in his dreams, and part of his personal journey requires him to be away. He hopes that Milli would understand this—that love can still thrive, even from a distance. But as the weeks pass, he can sense that Milli is increasingly dissatisfied with the setup. Their conversations reveal this tension. When Milli expresses her frustration about the distance, Nahar feels conflicted. He explains how much he cares for her, how deeply committed he is, and how he plans to bridge the gap between them with time. But Milli, who is more impulsive and emotionally driven, finds it difficult to accept the separation. While she enjoys the moments, they spend together when he's around, those moments are becoming less frequent. And in the times that he's gone, she feels lost, needing someone to fill that void.

Nahar begins to notice subtle changes in Milli's behaviour—delayed responses, vague excuses, and an apparent disinterest in keeping the emotional connection alive. She becomes more unpredictable, her moods fluctuating between being affectionate when he's around and indifferent when he's not. Nahar starts to suspect that perhaps Milli is drifting emotionally because she needs more than what he can give from afar. The weight of this realization hits him hard. What Nahar doesn't understand is how to reconcile this difference in their needs. For him, emotional connection should transcend physical proximity. He believes love can endure distance, but Milli wants more. She wants him there, physically. And when he isn't, Nahar fears that she starts seeking the emotional comfort he can't provide. This stark difference in how they view relationships is creating an invisible wedge, slowly pushing them apart. As much as Nahar loves Milli, he's beginning to accept that their relationship may not survive this fundamental difference. He doesn't want to lose her, but he's also not willing to sacrifice his personal journey or constantly compromise his own life to be there for her every moment. The fear that she may already be emotionally involved with someone else when he's not around lingers in his mind, but he chooses not to confront it directly.

Nahar's heart tells him to keep holding on, but his mind recognizes the truth: no matter how strong their connection is, Milli may never fully be content with a relationship that doesn't involve constant physical presence. And for Nahar, who sees love as something that can grow despite distance, this realization is heartbreaking. Nahar begins to sense a gradual deterioration in their relationship after the initial closeness they shared. Once, everything felt natural between them, filled with late-night conversations, shared laughter, and moments of intense connection. Now, however, Milli's behaviour grows erratic, her responses more distant, and arguments arise from the smallest issues. It starts subtly. Milli, who once cherished their late-night phone calls and eagerly updated Nahar about her day, now responds with curt messages. Excuses begin piling up — *"I'm busy," "I'll talk later," or "Something came up."* Initially, Nahar brushes it off, attributing it to the usual stresses of life. However, the pattern persists. Every conversation becomes a battlefield, with Milli criticizing Nahar over trivial matters. Whether it's about his lack of attention to minor details or misunderstandings about daily schedules, these issues balloon into heated arguments that leave Nahar feeling confused and frustrated.

The real problem lies in Milli's yearning for the independence she once had. Nahar begins to realize that she longs for the simplicity they had before they defined their relationship, back when things were casual, and neither of them felt the pressure to label what they shared. Milli's actions suggest that the emotional weight of their commitment is too much for her, and she subtly starts creating emotional distance to reclaim her sense of freedom. For Nahar, this is traumatic. He's someone who believes in the emotional depth of relationships and feels that once two people have defined their connection, it's something sacred. But it's becoming painfully clear that Milli doesn't hold the same values. Nahar starts to perceive that she may be getting bored with the relationship or at least disillusioned with the demands it brings. While he clings to the hope of resolving things, Milli seems to be slipping further away. As days pass, Nahar struggles with the emotional weight of being in a relationship where he's no longer sure if both of them are on the same page. The long-distance aspect further complicates things. Milli's attitude suggests she's not suited for maintaining a relationship without constant physical presence. She yearns for someone to be there, to fill the emotional gaps, but Nahar cannot always be there in person. His responsibilities, career ambitions, and personal commitments require him to be away at times, but the distance is clearly driving them apart. A painful realization dawns on Nahar: Milli might not be the kind of person who can maintain a long-distance relationship without becoming restless. He sees the signs clearly now

— her behaviour suggests that when he's not around, she's willing to entertain other possibilities. She's not the type to endure emotional absence or wait patiently for someone who's physically distant. In his heart, Nahar begins to fear that if he's not there to fill the emotional and physical space, Milli won't hesitate to find someone else who will. The space in their relationship widens as Milli starts to hint at wanting more freedom. The arguments escalate, but it's not about the topics they fight over; it's the underlying tension. Nahar can sense that Milli is pushing for a more casual arrangement, something less binding, less intense. It feels as though she's trying to undo the emotional ties they've built over time, hoping to return to a state where she's not obligated to anyone, where the relationship can be light and uncomplicated. For Nahar, this is gut-wrenching. His love for Milli runs deep, and he can't bear the thought of losing her.

Yet, he also knows he can't continue in a relationship where he constantly feels as though he's the only one holding on. The emotional imbalance is suffocating him. He's torn between his deep emotional connection to Milli and the growing realization that she might never be able to meet him at the same emotional level. This internal conflict leaves Nahar questioning everything. How much longer can he continue loving someone who might already have one foot out the door? How long can he compromise his own self-respect just to keep the relationship afloat? Every argument, every moment of Milli pulling away, chips away at his confidence in their future together. Yet, despite all the signs, Nahar can't bring himself to let go, even as the distance between them — both physical and emotional — continues to grow. Nahar begins to understand that confronting Milli about the changes in her behaviour will likely lead to more arguments, deepening the rift between them. He notices the subtle shifts in her demeanour — the delayed replies, the excuses for not spending time together, and the disinterest in the conversations that once brought them closer. Instead of reacting with anger or frustration, Nahar makes a conscious decision to handle things differently. He realizes that if he pushes her or continues to bring up his concerns, it will only make matters worse. So, Nahar chooses a quieter path. He starts maintaining a calm distance, retreating slowly from the emotional investment he once put into the relationship. He stops initiating conversations as frequently and doesn't chase after her when her attention fades. When Milli brings up small disagreements, he doesn't engage in the same way, choosing instead to remain composed, giving short responses, and letting her words pass without argument. Nahar realizes that by stepping back, he can observe more clearly what's happening between them, and in doing so, protect himself emotionally. This distance doesn't mean that Nahar has stopped caring for Milli, but he has accepted that pushing for more intimacy or clarity would only drive her further away. He knows that if their relationship is to survive, it needs balance, and right now, the imbalance is too great. Instead of constantly trying to fix things, Nahar adopts a more passive approach, allowing Milli the space she seems to be craving. By doing this, Nahar also gives himself the time to reflect. He starts focusing on other aspects of his life - his studies, his goals, and reconnecting with friends he might have neglected while he was so deeply absorbed in the relationship.

Though it's painful to admit, Nahar realizes that the more space he creates, the more he sees the truth of their situation. Milli is drifting, and though he doesn't want to lose her, he knows he can't force her to stay. In maintaining this calm distance, Nahar hopes that Milli will eventually notice the change and realize what's slipping away. He knows that only time will tell whether she will miss what they once had or continue to move away from him. For now, Nahar's strategy is one of quiet observation, of letting the relationship take its natural course, whether that means reconciliation or further separation. Nahar begins to feel a sense of relief and clarity after he starts maintaining emotional distance from Milli. Before this, the constant ups and downs of their relationship had taken a toll on him, leaving him feeling depressed and confused. He was caught in a loop of trying to fix things, apologizing for issues he didn't fully understand, and feeling helpless as Milli seemed to drift further away. It was exhausting, and he felt like he was losing himself in the process. Now, with some space between them, Nahar can see things more clearly. The haze of emotional confusion begins to lift, and he starts recognizing patterns in Milli's behaviour that he hadn't fully noticed before. He realizes that she had been inconsistent with her feelings, often pulling away and then coming back when it suited her. Nahar understands that he had been giving too much of himself, trying to hold on to someone who wasn't equally invested in the relationship. By distancing himself, Nahar regains a sense of control over his emotions and his life. He no longer feels like he's at the mercy of Milli's whims, and this makes him feel stronger, more in control of his own happiness. He understands now that her behaviour wasn't just about him — it reflected who she was as a person. She wasn't ready for the kind of commitment he desired, and she didn't value the relationship in the same way he did. This realization doesn't make Nahar bitter, but it does make him more aware. He understands that he can't change who Milli is, nor can he force someone to value a relationship the way he does. What he can control is how he reacts to it, and by maintaining his distance, he is prioritizing his own well-being. He feels great relief in this newfound clarity, recognizing that his worth isn't tied to whether Milli stays or goes. Nahar's emotional distance brings him peace, and with that peace, he begins to focus more on his own life.

He pours his energy into his studies, his goals, and reconnecting with friends. He becomes less anxious about Milli's responses, less tied to her behaviour, and more focused on his own growth. The weight that had once made him feel trapped in a cycle of disappointment and sadness starts to lift. Through this process, Nahar comes to understand that he had been holding on to an idea of who Milli was, rather than seeing her for who she truly is. The distance has given him the perspective he needed to see her flaws and understand that she wasn't the right partner for the kind of relationship he wanted. For the first time in a long while, Nahar feels free, and that sense of freedom brings him a deep sense of inner peace.

Chapter 22

Break from the Moods

A few days later, during one of their usual late-night conversations, Milli brings up the idea of going on a trip together. Her voice is light and excited as she talks about how much she needs a break and how fun it would be to get away for a while. However, Nahar isn't as enthusiastic as she is. His mind is preoccupied with his upcoming exams, and he knows he needs to focus on his studies. But there's something else weighing on him — he doesn't fully trust Milli anymore. Ever since their relationship became strained. And with Milli's indifferent behaviour and emotional distance, Nahar has started questioning whether she's truly committed to him. He's noticed the subtle shifts in her attitude, the way she seems distant, and how she finds reasons to argue over little things. The thought of her going on a trip alone makes him uneasy, especially after realizing that she's not the person he once thought she was. Although Nahar tries to focus on his priorities, the idea of Milli going on her own fills him with doubt. He doesn't want to be controlling, but deep down, he knows that if she goes without him, he'll be consumed with anxiety, fearing what she might do or who she might meet. His trust in her is fragile now, and the idea of her being in a new place, free to make her own decisions without his presence, unsettles him. Caught between his need to focus on his exam preparations and his lingering doubts about Milli's loyalty, Nahar hesitates. He doesn't want to outright refuse her, but he also knows he can't fully commit to the trip without sacrificing his study time. He pauses for a moment and carefully crafts his response. "I don't know if I can go right now," Nahar says, trying to keep his tone light. "You know I have exams coming up, and I really need to focus. But maybe we can plan something after?" Milli pushes back, her voice sounding a little disappointed but insistent. "We won't be gone for long. Just a weekend trip or something. You deserve a break too, Nahar. It's been a while since we've spent real time together". Nahar feels the pressure mounting. On one hand, he doesn't want to come across as overly cautious or controlling, but on the other, the cracks in their relationship have left him feeling vulnerable. He can't shake the fear that this trip might give her the freedom to stray, even if it's just emotionally. He takes a deep breath and replies, "I get that, but right now I can't afford to take any distractions. We'll definitely plan something after the exams are over.

I really want us to do that, but for now, I need to stay focused." Milli goes quiet for a moment, and Nahar wonders if she senses his hesitation, if she can feel the underlying mistrust in his voice. After a pause, she replies, "Alright, I get it. But let's plan something soon". Nahar agrees, relieved that the conversation ends without a fight. But deep inside, he knows that the underlying issue hasn't been resolved. His trust in Milli is still shaky, and though he's managed to dodge the trip for now, the future of their relationship remains uncertain. As much as he doesn't want to admit it, the cracks between them are growing, and no number of trips or distractions will be able to patch them up if the foundation isn't there. Nahar, feeling the tension between them, decides that maybe a break from everything could help restore their relationship. Though his exams are important, he can sense that things with Milli are at a tipping point. He doesn't want to lose her and perhaps a change of scenery could help them reconnect. During their conversation, Nahar hesitates for a moment before suggesting an alternative. "What if we go for a trek instead? Something different. I think it might give us a chance to clear our heads and enjoy some time together. I can manage my studies around it." Milli pauses, seemingly surprised by his sudden willingness to compromise. She's been pushing for them to spend time together, and this feels like a step in the right direction. "A trek sounds mesmerising," she says, her voice softening. "It's been a while since we've done something adventurous. Are you sure though? I know your exams are coming up." Nahar nods, although he feels a slight unease in his chest. He knows how crucial his studies are, but part of him hopes this trek will help them escape the problems that have been building between them. "I'll make it work," he says with a smile. "We both need this. I think it'll help us forget about all the stress for a while." In the screen behind, Nahar is also hoping that the trek will give them the chance to reconnect emotionally and physically. They had been through so many ups and downs recently, with the constant arguments and Milli's growing distance. He feels that if they can just get away from everything, the fresh air and natural beauty of the trek might bring them back to the closeness they once shared. For Milli, the idea of a trek seems exciting and a welcome distraction from the ongoing friction in their relationship. While she's happy that Nahar is agreeing to spend time with her, there's still a part of her that feels restless. However, she pushes those thoughts aside and agrees to the plan. As they start preparing for the trek, Nahar focuses on the hope that this trip will settle all the clashes.

He believes that maybe the outdoor adventure, the quiet, and the simplicity of being away from the world will remind them both why they fell in love in the first place. He's willing to sacrifice his time and energy in the hope of repairing what's broken. The upcoming trek represents more than just a getaway for Nahar-it's a last attempt to bring stability to a relationship that feels like it's slipping away. He's willing to go the extra mile, hoping the time together in the wilderness will either rekindle the flame or give him the clarity he needs about the future of their relationship. Nahar, eager to plan the trek, turns to Milli and asks, "So, which trek do you think would be good for both of us? Something that's not too hard but still gives us a nice adventure". Milli, after thinking for a moment, suggests, "How about Rudra Nath? It's a moderate trek, not too expensive, and I've heard it's really beautiful. Plus, it's not overcrowded like some other places." Nahar agrees, feeling a sense of relief that they've chosen something feasible. "Rudra Nath sounds perfect. I've read about it-it's challenging enough to be interesting, but not too tough for us to handle. And the views there are supposed to be incredible". They both sit down and start looking up the details, reading about the trek's moderate difficulty, the serene beauty of the surrounding mountains, and the spiritual significance of the destination. The trek seemed like a perfect balance-affordable, serene and so pacific, exactly what they both needed to clear their minds and reconnect. Nahar adds, "Plus, it's good for our budget right now. We can make it work without breaking the bank". Milli smiles, satisfied with the plan. "Yeah, and it's not too far either. We can just take it slow, enjoy the journey, and not rush. I think it'll be a great escape for us". The Rudra Nath trek, known for its stunning views and peaceful atmosphere, seems like the perfect place for them to reconnect away from the pressures of daily life. Both of them feel a sense of excitement as they finalize their plans. They hope that this trek will not only give them some adventure but also help them find the peace and clarity they desperately need in their relationship. As the date for the trek approaches, Nahar feels a mix of hope and nervousness. He's ready to make this trek a turning point for them, to leave behind the arguments and the tension and focus on rebuilding their bond. Nahar's decision to go on the Rudra Nath trek with Milli and their friends brings a new dynamic to their relationship.

Initially, Nahar hoped that this break would help resolve the growing tension between them. He was hesitant at first but eventually agreed to include their friends, thinking it might make the trip more enjoyable and less intense. As the trek approaches, Nahar remains focused on his studies but also makes time to plan the trip. The inclusion of friends introduces an element of uncertainty, as Nahar hopes the presence of others might alleviate any lingering doubts he has about Milli's commitment. However, he can't shake the feeling that Milli's request to include others could be her way of avoiding deeper intimacy with him. This trek becomes a pivotal moment, offering Nahar a chance to observe Milli in a different environment and gauge whether they can still find a connection amidst the cracks that have formed in their relationship. The journey to Rudra Nath will test both their bond and Nahar's resolve as he navigates the complexities of trust, love, and the desire for clarity in his relationship with Milli.

Nahar reached out to his friends, hopeful that they would be able to join him and Milli on the trek. However, one by one, they all responded that they were too busy with their own work or commitments. Ragini and Sudiksha had just started new jobs, and Sumit was traveling for his own exams and Ruhi had been a distant element these days in Nahar's and others lives. Nahar was disappointed but not entirely surprised, knowing how everyone's lives had become more complicated since their carefree days of studying together. Adesh, on the other hand, was interested in the trek. Despite his own busy schedule, he had always been the spontaneous one in the group, willing to make time for an adventure. He quickly agreed, excited at the prospect of getting away and spending time with Nahar and Milli. It felt like old times again, and Nahar found comfort in knowing that at least Adesh would be joining them. It gave him a sense of familiarity and support amidst the uncertainty of his relationship with Milli. Milli was already familiar with Adesh, as they had studied together in the past, so she was comfortable with the idea of him joining them. This relieved Nahar, knowing that there wouldn't be any awkwardness in their small group. He noticed that Milli seemed more relaxed now that their friends were no longer part of the trek, and he wondered if she had hoped for a smaller group from the beginning. Milli's friends were also unavailable due to their work commitments, so the group was finalized—just the three of them: Nahar, Milli, and Adesh.

Chapter 23

Plan of Action

The trio's trip felt manageable, even if it wasn't the private, romantic getaway Nahar had initially imagined. He reassured himself that the presence of a third person might take some of the pressure off and make the trek more enjoyable for everyone. After confirming that it would just be Nahar, Milli, and Adesh, they wasted no time in booking the Rudra Nath trek. The trek was scheduled for a month later, and the anticipation began to build as the days slowly passed. Nahar could feel the excitement bubbling within him, a mix of eagerness to escape into the serene mountains and hope that this trip might bring clarity and peace to the tension that had recently crept into his relationship with Milli. The group chat they created to plan the trek was filled with lively discussions. Adesh, ever the energetic one, frequently shared memes about hiking and adventure, making jokes about how unprepared they all were for the uphill challenge. Milli contributed as well, sharing tips on packing efficiently and ensuring they had everything they needed. Though their day-to-day communication had become somewhat distant, Nahar was grateful that planning the trek seemed to bring Milli back to her usual self, if only for brief moments. Nahar, meanwhile, kept a low profile, dividing his time between his exam preparation and checking off items from his trek checklist. In the back of his mind, he hoped the fresh air and natural beauty of the Rudra Nath trek would clear the fog that had settled between him and Milli. He was banking on this break to reset things, to bring back the easy, affectionate connection they once had. As the trek day neared, the excitement grew stronger. Nahar could see the growing excitement in Milli as well, which reassured him that she was equally invested in making this trip special. They had planned everything down to the last detail-gear, snacks, itineraries, and even a playlist to keep the mood light on the bus ride to the starting point. Each day, as Nahar studied or talked briefly with Milli, the trek loomed closer, a beacon of hope that maybe, just maybe, this adventure could bring them closer and help resolve the lingering tension. With each passing day, the countdown felt more significant-both for the thrill of the journey and what it might mean for their relationship.

With just a few days left before the trek, Nahar, Milli, and Adesh found themselves in a whirlwind of excitement and preparation. None of them had expected that they would actually commit to such an adventure, which added an extra layer of excitement to the experience. The spontaneous decision to go on the Rudra Nath trek had turned into something more real with every passing day, and now, with their tickets already booked, all that remained was the anticipation of the day itself. Nahar could feel the shift in the air as he packed his bag, carefully folding his clothes and making sure his hiking gear was in order. Every item he placed into his backpack felt like a step closer to something transformative-whether for the adventure itself or the state of his relationship with Milli. The usual tension between them seemed to have dissipated a little, as both of them were now fully focused on the trek. Milli, too, was excited. Her messages were frequent, asking Nahar and Adesh about last-minute details-whether they had enough snacks, if they'd remembered to pack extra socks, or if they should bring a camera to capture the views along the way. Her enthusiasm was infectious, and it reminded Nahar of how things used to be between them when everything felt simpler. Adesh, always the joker, kept things light in their group chat, teasing Nahar about how he'd handle the trek and joking about how they'd probably all end up lost in the mountains without a map. His carefree attitude balanced out Nahar's more reflective mood, and Milli's steady excitement kept them all motivated. The spontaneity of the whole thing added an unexpected thrill to the preparations. None of them had initially expected to go on a trek like this, which made every little detail of planning feel more exciting. The idea that this adventure was just around the corner, something they hadn't planned months in advance, made it feel even more special. They had no idea what to expect, which only heightened the sense of wonder. As the final days approached, Nahar found himself looking forward to more than just the breath-taking mountain views. He hoped this trek would bring him clarity about Milli, about their relationship, and about the next steps in his life. It wasn't just an adventure into nature; it was an adventure into the unknown parts of himself and his connection with Milli.

The day they had all been waiting for had finally arrived. Excitement buzzed in the air as Nahar hurriedly packed the last of his gear, double-checking to make sure he hadn't forgotten anything essential. The trek to Rudra Nath was about to begin, and this adventure felt like a much-needed escape for all of them.

Chapter 24

An Expedition Towards the Trek

Milli and Adesh had already left from their respective cities, boarding the same train. Nahar was the last one to join them, and as usual, time wasn't on his side. He was running late. His heart raced as he checked his watch repeatedly, calculating how much time he had before the train would arrive at his station. Somehow, despite the last-minute rush, he managed to gather everything and head for the railway station.

He arrived at the station with just enough time to spare. The train hadn't arrived yet, and a wave of relief washed over him. Nahar stood there, adjusting the straps on his backpack, scanning the platform for any signs of Adesh and Milli. The platform was crowded with people, a mix of locals and travellers, but in that moment, Nahar's mind was focused solely on the journey ahead.

He took a deep breath, feeling the weight of both excitement and nervous anticipation. This trek was important for many reasons. It wasn't just about the adventure—it was also an opportunity to reconnect with Milli, to resolve the lingering tension between them, and to find out what this experience would mean for their relationship. The uncertainty of it all was unsettling, but there was a sense of hope that maybe, just maybe, this trip would bring them closer.

Soon, the train pulled into the station, its horn echoing through the platform. Nahar quickly checked his seat number and hopped aboard, making his way through the crowded aisles. After what felt like an eternity, he spotted Adesh and Milli, who were already settled into their seats.

"There he is, Mr. Always-on-Time!" Adesh teased, grinning as Nahar approached them.

Milli smiled warmly when she saw Nahar, and for a moment, it felt like the tension between them had vanished.

"Cutting it close as usual," Milli added with a playful tone, though there was a flicker of something deeper in her eyes, something that Nahar couldn't quite place. Maybe it was excitement, or maybe it was the uncertainty that still hung between them.

Nahar slid into his seat next to Milli, giving her a small nod and a half-smile, while Adesh continued cracking jokes to lighten the mood. The train started to move, slowly picking up speed as it carried them away from the city, toward the mountains and the unknown adventures that awaited them.

As the scenery began to change outside the window, Nahar felt a strange mix of excitement and apprehension. This trek was a break from everything-the studying, the city, the complicated dynamics between him and Milli. He hoped that the mountains would bring clarity, and maybe, by the time they return, things between him and Milli would be clearer too.

For now, though, he let himself enjoy the moment. The rhythmic hum of the train, the warmth of Milli sitting beside him, and the banter with Adesh felt like a good start to what promised to be an unforgettable journey.

As Nahar settled into his seat, feeling the energy of the journey, he couldn't help but notice the shared excitement among the three of them. It had been a while since they'd all done something like this together, and the anticipation of the trek to Rudra Nath was palpable.

Suddenly, a young man, probably around Nahar's age, seated a few rows away, glanced over at them and smiled. He must have noticed their lively conversation and excited moods.

"Hey, you all look like you're heading somewhere fun. What's the reason behind all this excitement?" he asked, leaning slightly forward with curiosity.

Nahar exchanged a quick look with Adesh and Milli, and then replied with a grin, "We're heading to Rudra Nath for a trek. Been planning this for a while, and we're finally on our way. Can't wait to hit the trails!"

The young man's face lit up with enthusiasm. "No way! I'm going to Rudra Nath too!" he said, his eyes widening with surprise and amazement "I've been looking forward to this trek for months."

Milli, who had been listening, smiled and said, "That's awesome! Small world, huh? Looks like we're all in for the same adventure."

Adesh, ever the conversationalist, chimed in, "Looks like we're going to have some company on the trek. What are the odds?"

The young man moved closer, introducing himself as Sarthak. As they began talking, it became clear that Sarthak was as excited as they were, if not more. He shared how this trek had been on his bucket list for a while and how he had planned it as a solo trip, hoping to meet new people along the way.

"Well, looks like you won't be trekking alone anymore," Nahar said with a smile. "The more, the merrier."

They spent the next hour exchanging stories and discussing the upcoming trek. Sarthak shared tips from his previous treks, and Nahar and Adesh filled him in on their plans for Rudra Nath. The mood in the group became even more lively, the shared excitement now amplified by the serendipity of meeting another trekker headed to the same destination.

As the train chugged along through the countryside, Nahar glanced at Milli, who seemed more relaxed now, her earlier tension from the past weeks dissolving in the excitement of the moment. This trek was becoming more than just a getaway-it was a chance to reset, not just for Nahar and Milli but for everyone involved.

With each passing moment, their anticipation grew. Rudra Nath was not just a destination—it was the start of something new.

As the train stopped at a mid-way station, a lively group of boys hopped on, carrying musical instruments—guitars, drums, and even a violin. They were on their way to participate in a national-level music competition. Their energy was contagious, and soon the entire compartment was buzzing with excitement.

One of the boys, a guitarist, strummed a few chords, warming up. The drummer tapped along lightly on the armrest, syncing effortlessly. Soon, they launched into a full-fledged rehearsal, their harmonies filling the space. Nahar, Milli, Adesh, and Sarthak exchanged glances, and without a second thought, they joined in, clapping along and humming to the melodies.

Milli, always full of enthusiasm, couldn't resist singing along. Her voice blended well with the boys' harmonies, surprising Nahar, who watched her with admiration. Adesh, typically quiet, found himself tapping his feet and even joined in the chorus, his face lit up with joy. Sarthak, who had only recently joined the group, found this spontaneous musical moment to be the perfect icebreaker, and he chimed in with a low, steady hum.

The boys appreciated the support and invited the group to join their rehearsal. Together, they sang classic songs, folk tunes, and even some upbeat, contemporary hits. The entire compartment was soon filled with music, laughter, and camaraderie.

Nahar felt a sense of warmth in this unexpected moment, bonding not only with Milli and Adesh but also with these strangers who shared a common love for music and adventure.

The train rattled on through the countryside, passing by fields, rivers, and distant mountain ranges, the sound of the violin weaving through the hum of the wheels. The music echoed through the cabin, turning the journey into a celebration. By the end of the rehearsal, everyone was clapping and cheering, feeling like old friends despite having just met.

This spontaneous experience made the anticipation of the trek more luscious. For Nahar, it was a reminder of how life's unexpected moments often turn into the best memories. As the train sped towards their destination, the group of travellers—each heading toward their own adventures—felt connected by the shared experience of music, excitement, and the open road ahead.

As the train pulled into the next station, the group of boys prepared to leave. They gathered their instruments, waved goodbye, and wished Nahar, Milli, Adesh, and Sarthak good luck on their trek. Everyone exchanged warm smiles, and the music group disappeared into the platform, leaving behind the echo of their melodies and good memories.

It was now evening, and the air outside was growing cooler as the sun set. Nahar, Adesh, Milli, and Sarthak decided it was time for dinner. They had packed some simple meals, and after settling back into their seats, they served out the food for them. Sarthak, now fully the part of the group, had also brought some snacks and offered them to everyone, completing the impromptu dinner setup.

As they ate together, the conversation flowed easily. They spoke about their excitement for the trek, sharing thoughts on what they might encounter along the way. Sarthak, being new to the group, fit in well, adding his own stories of past adventures and making everyone laugh with his witty remarks.

The dinner was simple-rice, chapati, some packed vegetables, and snacks—but the company made it feel more special.

Nahar looked around, feeling content. He had been unsure about this trip at first, especially with the recent tensions between him and Milli, but in this moment, surrounded by friends and laughter, he felt grateful for the decision.

As the train continued its journey through the evening, the group enjoyed the relaxed atmosphere, the rhythm of the train, and the promise of adventure ahead. They all knew that this trek would be more than just a physical journey; it would be an experience filled with memories and bonding that would stay with them for a long time.

After finishing their dinner, the group settled into their seats, ready to rest for the night. The rhythmic sound of the train on the tracks lulled them into sleep one by one, as they anticipated the journey ahead. Nahar lay back, feeling the gentle sway of the train and imagining the excitement of the trek they were about to embark on. By morning, the train arrived at their destination, and the group, still groggy from sleep, got off the train. They found a small café near the station where they freshened up and had breakfast, keeping the mood light with jokes and conversation. The air was crisp, a reminder that they were nearing the mountains, and the excitement started to build again.

After breakfast, they made their way to the bus station to catch the bus that would take them to the base of the Rudra Nath trek. As they boarded the crowded bus, Nahar hoped to sit with Milli and share the moment with her. However, because of the rush of passengers and limited seats, Milli ended up sitting with Adesh, while Sarthak took the seat next to Nahar. It wasn't what Nahar had envisioned, but he smiled and adjusted, knowing the trek would give them plenty of time together.

As the bus rolled out of the station, Nahar glanced over at Milli and Adesh, who were deep in conversation. He could feel a slight twinge of disappointment but quickly brushed it off. Sarthak, sitting beside him, struck up a conversation about the trek, the different routes they could take, and the best ways to prepare for the high altitude. It helped Nahar focus on the adventure rather than his expectations for the trip.

The bus ride was long, winding through mountain roads that grew narrower and steeper as they climbed higher.

Nahar looked out the window, taking in the majestic views of the mountains, valleys, and rivers below. He knew that this journey was not just about the trek, but also about resetting the dynamics between him and Milli, and perhaps even finding some clarity in their relationship.

Chapter 25

Deep Jerk in Ananthur

After a long, winding bus ride through the mountain roads, they finally reached the quaint town of Ananthur just as the evening sun cast a golden hue over the landscape. The town was nestled amidst towering peaks, its narrow streets bustling with a mix of locals and travellers. The cool mountain breeze greeted them as they stepped off the bus, a welcome contrast to the warm, stuffy air inside.

Nahar, Milli, Adesh, and Sarthak gathered their bags, their bodies tired from the long journey but their spirits still high with excitement for the trek ahead. They needed to find a hotel to rest for the night before their trek began in the morning. The town was small, and accommodation options were limited. They roamed the streets for a while, checking out different places, most of which were already full with other trekkers preparing for their own journeys.

After some efforts and inquiries, they finally found a modest hotel with one room available. The room was simply unadorned though cosy with two wooden beds and a small window overlooking the town. The décor was basic but clean, and after such a long trip, it felt like a little slice of comfort.

"This will do," Adesh said, throwing his bag on one of the beds. "We'll be out exploring most of the evening anyway."

They quickly freshened up, the cool water washing away the fatigue from the road. After changing into fresh clothes, they were ready to explore Ananthur. The trek was set to begin early the next morning, so this evening would be their only chance to experience the charm of the town before heading into the wilderness.

Stepping out into the crisp evening air, the group made their way through the narrow streets, which were illuminated by warm, golden streetlights. Small shops lined the cobblestone paths, selling everything from handmade trinkets and souvenirs to trekking gear and local snacks. The scent of roasted chestnuts and sizzling momos filled the air, mingling with the fresh mountain breeze.

Milli seemed more relaxed than she had been in days. Sarthak and Adesh led the way, talking about their excitement for the trek and discussing their strategy for the climb. Nahar, though absorbed in the beauty of the town. The group wandered into a local café, its wooden benches and low-hanging lights giving it a warm, rustic atmosphere. They ordered hot cups of chai and a variety of local dishes—momos, thukpa, and a few spicy mountain delicacies. The warmth of the food and drink eased the weariness of travel and filled them with renewed energy.

As they sat around the table after dinner, they continued their exploration, walking through the hushed streets of Ananthur, the sky now a deep indigo, dotted with stars. They passed by an old temple at the edge of the town, its stone steps worn smooth by centuries of pilgrims. The town had an old-world charm, and the mountains surrounding them seemed to stand as silent sentinels, watching over the town and its visitors.

The walk helped clear their minds, and the tension that had been simmering between Nahar and Milli seemed to fade with each step. Nahar felt a sense of calm wash over him, the beauty of the place and the presence of his friends reminding him of the simple joys of life.

By the time they returned to their hotel room, the town being restful, down for the night, the blank streets paving for a few late-night wanderers and the occasional distant bark of a dog. They settled into their room, discussing their plans for the trek. The excitement for the next day—the beginning of their 4-night, 5-day adventure into the wild—was palpable.

The room was small, with only two beds. Adesh, Sarthak, and Nahar settled on one bed, leaving Milli on the other. They chatted and laughed, the camaraderie lightening the mood. Adesh suggested they play a round of *Dumb Charades* to kill time, and soon, the room was filled with laughter and guesses as they threw themselves into the game. Nahar participated, but he began to feel the exhaustion of the day setting in. His mind wandered for a moment as he looked at Milli, who seemed to be in high spirits after a long day of exploration. She suggested that they watch a documentary she had heard about—a real-life story that had intrigued her for some time.

"Let's watch it together!" Milli suddenly said, her eyes bright with excitement. "Come on, there's enough space here," she added, looking at the bed where Nahar, Adesh, and Sarthak were sitting.

Before Nahar could process the situation, Milli stood up and walked over to their bed. Without hesitation, she settled down between him and Adesh, grabbing the remote as if it was the most natural thing to do. Sarthak shifted a little to make space, and soon, they were all squeezed onto the bed, ready to watch the documentary.

But for Nahar, this moment wasn't comfortable. It felt awkward, almost surreal. He had never been in such close proximity to Milli while surrounded by others, especially in such an intimate setting. His mind raced as he tried to make sense of what was happening. His discomfort grew, as it was a stark contrast to the boundaries they had previously maintained. Milli was acting casually, but to Nahar, it felt like a shift—something has changed.

As the documentary played on the small TV in the room, Nahar found it difficult to focus. He felt hyper-aware of Milli's presence next to him. Her shoulder brushed against his arm, and though it seemed innocent, the moment carried weight for Nahar. His thoughts spiralled. Was this just a casual moment, or was Milli testing the boundaries between them? Had the dynamic between them subtly shifted without him realizing it?

For Milli, it seemed like a carefree moment of fun. But for Nahar, this was the turning point. A line had been crossed, one that had always existed between them. He could sense that something deeper was happening beneath the surface. The playful interactions that once defined their relationship were now entangled in a web of unspoken feelings, blurred boundaries, and hidden tension. Nahar's mind was filled with doubts, not just about this moment, but about the future of their relationship.

As they sat there, watching the documentary, Nahar couldn't help but wonder if this closeness, this casual intimacy, was what Milli had wanted all along. Did she crave a kind of freedom that he couldn't fully provide from a distance? Or was this simply a fleeting moment of spontaneity?

The rest of the group seemed to be enjoying the documentary, completely unaware of the inner conflict brewing within Nahar. As Milli's focus remained on the screen, Nahar's thoughts drifted, pulling him further into uncertainty about the direction of their relationship.

This was no longer just a trek or a simple trip. For Nahar, this was the beginning of something different—a shift that would challenge everything he had come to believe about their relationship.

After watching about half of the documentary, the group gradually began to drift off to sleep, still cramped together on the small bed. The room fell into silence, broken only by the quiet hum of the TV still playing in the background. Nahar lay there, wide awake, unable to shut off the thoughts racing through his mind. His body was pressed against Milli's, with Adesh and Sarthak on the other side, but there was no sense of warmth in this closeness for him.

He couldn't understand how Milli seemed so unaffected, so comfortable, casually sharing a bed with all three of them. She hadn't hesitated, hadn't thought twice about it, as if it was just a regular moment between friends. But for Nahar, this wasn't normal. The emotional turmoil within him was undeniable. Every small action, every detail, fed into his growing doubts and confusion.

He began to wonder if Milli even felt the same intensity of connection that he did. Did their relationship mean as much to her as it did to him?

The ease with which she shared such intimate moments with others made him question whether she was as deeply invested. Perhaps it was his own fault for wanting more, for expecting something deeper than what she was prepared to give. He had convinced himself that this trip would bring them closer, that it would ease the tension that had been simmering for months. But now, it felt like the cracks were deepening.

As Milli slept peacefully beside him, oblivious to the emotional storm brewing within him, Nahar stared at the ceiling, lost in his thoughts. Her actions—sleeping with three men in one bed, without a second thought— had struck at the heart of his feelings for her. It wasn't about jealousy or possession. It was about trust and understanding, and the realization that perhaps they were not on the same page about what their relationship truly meant.

After what felt like hours of lying there in emotional turmoil, Nahar could no longer take it. He gently shifted, careful not to wake anyone, and slowly pulled himself out of the bed. He stood for a moment, looking at Milli,

Adesh, and Sarthak, all fast asleep, before making his way to the empty bed on the other side of the room.

As he settled down on the empty bed, a wave of loneliness washed over him. The space between him and Milli felt bigger than ever. He had always been the one to accommodate, to make excuses for her behaviour, to forgive and move forward. But tonight, something had changed. He was beginning to realize that no matter how much he tried, he couldn't ignore the growing distance between them—physically and emotionally.

The room was dark and quiet now, but Nahar's mind was still loud, filled with doubts, frustrations, and unspoken words. He stared out the window at the night sky, feeling utterly disconnected from the girl he had once felt so close to. Perhaps this was the start of something he had feared all along—a slow unravelling of their relationship, where love alone wasn't enough to keep them together.

For the first time in a long time, Nahar felt unsure of the future with Milli.

As Nahar settled into the empty bed, trying to calm his restless thoughts, the room began to feel suffocating. The weight of his emotions, the confusion, and the growing distance between him and Milli overwhelmed him. Lying there, he felt a lump in his throat, and before he could stop himself, tears began to roll down his cheeks.

He tried to stifle his sobs, not wanting to wake anyone, but the emotional pain was too strong. He had never imagined that Milli, the person he loved so deeply, could make him feel so isolated and misunderstood.

Nahar replayed the night in his mind so as to once again reassess and re-evaluate himself if he was right towards what he was recently feeling so unnatural about. The carefree way through which Milli had invited herself to the bed with the others, without considering Nahar's want to have the space with her and ignoring away the unsaid love and longingness Nahar was expecting her to. Her lack of awareness of how much it was hurting him, made him question everything. How could she be so blind to his feelings? How could she not feel the emotional boundaries that seemed so important to him? It wasn't about the physical act of sleeping beside others— it was the emotional disconnection, the disregard for the sensitivity and respect he craved in their relationship. The stark realization that perhaps she didn't understand him, neither she cared for it, the way he thought she did, hit him hard.

The more Nahar thought about it, the more suffocated he felt. His heart ached, and he could no longer bear to stay in that room. Quietly, he slipped out of bed and stood up, glancing at Milli once more. She was still asleep, unaware of the storm raging inside him. Nahar's chest tightened as he realized that she probably wouldn't even notice his absence.

Without a second thought, he grabbed his jacket, put on his shoes, and quietly left the room. The hallway outside was dark and empty, but he welcomed the quiet solitude. As soon as he stepped outside, the cold night air hit him, and he felt a brief moment of relief from the suffocation that had consumed him moments ago.

Nahar started walking, not really knowing where he was going but needing to escape, to clear his head. The streets were nearly deserted, the occasional sound of distant cars or the rustling of leaves breaking the silence. His footsteps echoed on the pavement, grounding him as he tried to make sense of his emotions.

Tears continued to stream down his face as he walked through the dark streets, his heart heavy with the weight of disappointment and sadness. He felt betrayed—not by any particular action, but by the growing realization that Milli might never be the person he had imagined her to be. He had built her up in his mind, believed in their connection, but now it seemed like she wasn't capable of meeting him at the same emotional depth. Nahar had been willing to forgive, to accommodate, to hold on despite everything, but how long could he keep doing that without losing himself in the process?

The further he walked, the calmer his thoughts became. The cold air felt refreshing against his tear-streaked face, but it didn't numb the ache inside. Nahar felt like he was at a crossroads, unsure of what the future held for him and Milli. He wanted to hold on to the love they had shared, but he couldn't ignore the growing cracks in their relationship.

He stopped for a moment, looking up at the sky. The stars shimmered above him, distant and cold, reminding him of how he felt in this moment—adrift, alone, and uncertain. For the first time, Nahar questioned whether this relationship was worth fighting for anymore. He wasn't sure if he could keep holding on to something that seemed to be slipping away, no matter how hard he tried.

Chapter 26

A Friendship Revival

After walking for what felt like hours, His heart still heavy, but a newfound resolve was forming inside him. He knew things couldn't continue as they were. Something had to change, and this trip might be the turning point. Whether it would bring them closer or push them apart, Nahar wasn't sure, but he knew he couldn't ignore the truth any longer.

As Nahar walked through the cold, empty streets, his mind a whirlwind of emotions, he felt an overwhelming need to talk to someone. He had been bottling up his feelings for too long, and tonight's events had pushed him to the edge. He couldn't keep it all inside anymore. Without thinking, he pulled out his phone and scrolled through his contacts until he found Ruhi's name. The person he would often go so as to validate hi actions, his thoughts or any other feeling. She had always been a good listener, someone who had known him before everything became so complicated with Milli.

He hesitated for a moment, unsure if calling her this late was a good idea. But the loneliness gnawed at him, and before he could overthink it, he hit the call button knowing and assuring himself as she too was on a trip with her friends and that she could in no time pick up his call. Ruhi had been quiet busy these months since she left for her job but never it happened that she ignored or left Nahar;s call unattended. Although after Milli's arrival into his life Nahar had been a secretive one and selective one and so wasn't that frequent with Ruhi on call or messages these months. Still having the faith in his friend, he gave a call to Ruhi to vomit out what he wasn't able to digest tonight about.

The phone rang a few times before Ruhi picked up, her voice sounding lively, unaware of the storm brewing in Nahar's heart.

"Nahar! How's it going? I heard you're off on a trek! That's awesome!" she said, her excitement evident.

Nahar's heart sank. He hadn't even thought about the trek in the last few hours; it seemed like a distant memory compared to what he was feeling right now. For a moment, he didn't know how to respond. He tried to muster some enthusiasm, but the words didn't come. His silence must have spoken volumes because Ruhi's tone shifted, her excitement dimming.

"Nahar? Is everything okay?" she asked, her voice filled with concern.

Nahar swallowed hard, trying to hold back the flood of emotions that threatened to spill over. He opened his mouth to speak, but nothing came out at first. Finally, after a long pause, he found the words.

"I... I don't know, Ruhi. I thought this trek would be something special, something that would bring me and Milli closer, but... everything feels so wrong," he confessed, his voice barely above a whisper.

Ruhi's concern deepened. "What's going on? Did something happen between you and Milli?"

And that was all it took. The dam broke, and Nahar began to tell her everything—about the way things had been disentangling between him and Milli for months, the arguments, the emotional distance, and how tonight, sleeping in the same bed as the others, had felt like the final blow. He told her how Milli's actions had hurt him deeply, how he had felt like a stranger in the relationship, and how he no longer trusted that she was the person he thought she was.

As Nahar poured his heart out, Ruhi listened peacefully, allowing him to release all the pain and confusion he had been carrying. She didn't interrupt, sensing that he needed to get it all out.

"I don't know what to do anymore," Nahar admitted, his voice trembling. "I love her, Ruhi. I really do. But this… it's breaking me. I feel like I'm the only one holding on, and I'm not sure if I can keep doing it."

Ruhi sighed softly, her voice gentle yet firm. "Nahar, I'm so sorry you're going through this. It sounds like you've been carrying a lot for a long time, and it's okay to feel lost. But you need to ask yourself what's more important—your peace or holding on to something that's hurting you?"

Her words hit him hard. Nahar knew Ruhi was right, but it wasn't as simple as letting go. His emotions for Milli ran deep, and the idea of a future without her felt unbearable. But at the same time, the weight of the relationship was crushing him.

"I just don't understand," Nahar said, his voice cracking. "How can someone be so close to you one moment and then feel so distant the next? How can she not see how much this is hurting me?"

Ruhi sighed again. "People change, Nahar. Sometimes, they don't even realize it themselves. It sounds like Milli doesn't fully understand the impact she's having on you. And maybe she's struggling with her own things. But you can't keep sacrificing your happiness and self-respect for someone else's sake. Relationships are supposed to be a two-way street."

Ruhi listened carefully, sensing the depth of his emotional damage he was now going through. She didn't offer solutions or quick fixes because she wanted Nahar himself to find solutions for him. According to her the best solution to one's own problems should come from one's own will and wisdom. Also she had been always warning Nahar regarding this as she noticed those certain changes in him which she knew aren't the sign of a pure and deep bonded love which are meant to last forever. She sensed through her strong intuitions that whatever was happening wasn't for good. She made him cautious towards those negative alleviations frequently from his end but as in love people forget which's the best food served to them, same was the situation with Nahar too. When Ruhi started making him look towards his flaws in his behaviour he started side-lining her and reduced the frequency of talks and chats with her. But as good friend of his when Nahar needed her she was there by him but wanted him to see through the fog himself now and so she asked him to get calm down first, rethink the objective of his journey to life now and then decide where to walk through. And thus she just left him with an open-ended solution so that he could feel contented. This didn't bring any answer for Nahar to come out through his pain he was going through but just being able to share his pain with someone made Nahar feel a little less alone. Nahar wiped his tears from his eyes, trying to regain his composure. "I know. I know you're right. But it's so hard, Ruhi, I don't want to lose her" replied Nahar.

"I get that," Ruhi replied softly. "But sometimes, holding on too tightly can cause more harm than good.

You deserve to be with someone who sees you, who values you, and who's willing to work through the tough times with you. If Milli isn't that person anymore, maybe it's time to ask yourself if this is what you really want."

Her words lingered in Nahar's mind as he continued walking while talking to her. She was in no mood to settle him down while he tried to escape from the situation putting himself in a state of unconsciousness. He knew she was offering him the tough love he needed, but it didn't make the reality any easier to face. He wasn't ready to give up, but he also couldn't keep going like this.

"Thanks, Ruhi," Nahar said in a low tone. "I needed to hear that, I needed you to hear me out, to be with me in all these. "I'm always here for you, Nahar. Just remember—you're stronger than you think to deal with the stuff like "Love". And whatever happens, you'll get through it", all you need is to think wisely and not being emotionally weak and acting as a fool.

After hanging up, Nahar felt a little lighter but the ache in his chest remained. Ruhi had given him the clarity but he still wasn't sure what his next step would be. All he knew was that something had to change.

As Nahar made his way back to the hotel, his phone buzzed again. This time, it was Sarthak calling, his voice filled with concern.

"Where are you, man? It's the middle of the night!" Sarthak sounding shocked asked Nahar.

Nahar, still feeling the weight of his thoughts, replied calmly, "I just went for a walk, needed some air. I'm coming back now, don't worry."

There was a pause on the other end, and Sarthak seemed to process the unusual situation. "A walk? At this hour? Alone? Dude, this place is not that familiar. You should've told me."

"I know, I know," Nahar said, his voice tired. "I'll be back in a few minutes. Just heading back to the hotel."

Sarthak didn't push the issue further, though the concern in his voice was obvious. "Alright, just get back safely. We don't know this place, man."

Nahar cut the call and quickened his pace. The hotel came into view, and as he stepped inside, he saw that everyone was awake by then. Sarthak, Adesh, and even Milli looked up as he entered, concern etched on their faces.

"Everything okay?" Sarthak asked, the first to speak.

Nahar forced a small smile, trying to downplay the situation. "Yeah, all good. Just needed some fresh air."

Adesh gave him a long look, sensing something more, but chose not to pry. Milli, however, stayed quiet, her eyes following Nahar as he settled into the room. There was an awkward tension in the air, unspoken but palpable.

Sarthak broke the silence, walking up to Nahar. "Listen, man, next time you need to head out, just let me know. I'll come with you. None of us really know this place, and it's not safe to go wandering around alone."

Nahar appreciated the gesture, though his mind was still miles away. "Yeah, sure. Thanks."

Nahar lay in the darkened room, his mind racing as the weight of the situation pressed down on him. The flicker of the TV had long since faded, and the muffled sound of his friends breathing deeply in their sleep only intensified his solitude. He couldn't understand how Milli could be so oblivious, so unaware of how her actions were affecting him.

Watching her laugh and joke earlier, sitting casually between Adesh and Sarthak, had been unsettling. It wasn't the proximity alone; it was the comfort with which she did it.

For Nahar, relationships were built on boundaries, and their closeness had always felt sacred—an unspoken bond that kept them unique, separate from others. Yet tonight, seeing Milli so easily blend into the group, so freely sharing her space with others without a single thought that before anybody else her time, her care, concern and longingness belonged to Nahar, shattered something inside him.

It wasn't just that she was sitting with them. It was how she did it. So natural, so effortless, as if it hadn't even crossed her mind that Nahar might feel uncomfortable. How could she not realize? How could she not sense the storm brewing inside him?

For Nahar, every small detail mattered. The way Milli hadn't hesitated to sit with them, her laughter that once seemed so genuine and warm now felt like a reminder of how far they'd drifted. He had always trusted her, believed in the sanctity of what they shared, but now... everything felt distorted. His mind wandered to deeper doubts, wondering if she ever truly valued their relationship the way he did. He wanted to be her saviour in the group, for her discomforts, her awkwardness and her emotional insecurity as this was what supposed to be in that situation that generally happens with people deeply in love when they are in public or among others and what generally happens in these kinds of affairs.

Lying there, staring at the ceiling, Nahar's thoughts spiralled further. He started to replay their past interactions, searching for signs he might have missed. Every moment of tension, every argument they'd had over the past few months, resurfaced. It all seemed to lead to this point. Perhaps Milli wasn't capable of sustaining a meaningful, long-distance relationship. Maybe she craved attention, company, even if it wasn't from him.

Nahar had always been willing to overlook her occasional distant behaviour, always quick to apologize even when it wasn't his fault. But now, seeing her this different, it struck him how different they truly were. For him, this relationship meant everything—it was deeply personal, something sacred. But for her? It felt as though she could switch roles, blend with others without a second thought. The thought gnawed at him-if he wasn't around, could she so easily be with someone else?

His mind, once full of affection and hope, began to fill with accusations. Was she capable of replacing him? Could she just move on, without hesitation, if he wasn't there?

These questions haunted him, replaying over and over, as if some inner voice was whispering the painful truth he wasn't ready to accept. Milli was starting to feel distant, both emotionally and now physically.

The discomfort of the situation was suffocating. Nahar's sense of betrayal grew stronger, and with it, a creeping realization: Milli didn't seem to hold their relationship with the same depth that he did. For her, it seemed casual, easily swayed by the people around her.

But for Nahar, it was everything—his emotional anchor in the turbulence of his life.

His trust in Milli, once so unshakeable, now felt fragile. He couldn't help but feel like she was slipping away from him, and worse, that she didn't even care. Her actions tonight, however small or innocent they might seem to others, had cracked something inside him. This wasn't just a random night of discomfort—it was the culmination of months of doubt and suspicion. Nahar realized that Milli he once knew, the girl he had fallen so deeply in love with, wasn't the same anymore.

Or perhaps, she had never been that girl and he had just failed to see it.

As Nahar sat on the empty bed, his mind still reeling from the night's revelations, he remembered Ruhi's words from their phone conversation. Her voice echoed in his head: "Don't let the trek turn into a bad memory because of her. You deserve this experience, Nahar."

Ruhi had always been a voice of reason in his life. She had known both Milli and Adesh, but even she couldn't anticipate Adesh's betrayal. Nahar could sense the disappointment in Ruhi's tone when they spoke. She was upset, not just with Milli but with Adesh as well. Adesh had always been a good friend—loyal, trustworthy. But what he did tonight had shattered that trust, and Nahar knew Ruhi would be just as heartbroken about it as he was.

Still, Ruhi's advice rang true. "Don't let this ruin the trek." Nahar had been looking forward to this trip, and deep down, he didn't want to walk away from it with only bitterness in his heart.

He knew he had to find a way to salvage the experience, to enjoy it for what it was supposed to be—a break from life, an adventure, a chance to reconnect with nature and himself.

Nahar took a deep breath, collecting the courage he knew he needed to move forward. This trek doesn't belong to Milli. It doesn't belong to Adesh. It was his trek, and he wouldn't let them take it away from him. He realized that no matter whatever had happened with Milli or Adesh, he had the power to make this a positive experience.

One thought kept him grounded: *Sarthak.* The young man they'd met on the train had quickly become like a brother to Nahar. In the short time they had spent together, Sarthak had proven to be good-natured, genuine, and supportive. Their bond had grown naturally, and Nahar felt a sense of relief knowing that he could count on Sarthak. He wasn't alone in this, after all.

As Nahar gathered his thoughts, he decided. He would focus at the encouraging resolution, towards the favourable conclusion. He would emphasize on Sarthak's company and make the trek about growth, exploration, and healing. He would compartmentalize the pain he was feeling and not let it define his experience. Ruhi was right—this didn't have to become an unpleasant recollection. This could still be indelible.

The next morning, Nahar woke up with a renewed sense of purpose. He was still hurt, still disappointed, but he wasn't going to let those feelings consume him. As they prepared to leave for the trek, he found himself gravitating towards Sarthak, appreciating his whimsical humour and lively amusement. They laughed, shared stories, and in those moments, Nahar felt a sense of freedom that he hadn't felt in a long time.

While Milli and Adesh continued with their own dynamic, Nahar's focal point was Sarthak and the adventure ahead. He didn't avoid them, but he no longer let their presence dictate his mood. Every step they took on the trail became a step towards healing. The fresh air, the stunning views, and the physical challenge of the trek all gave Nahar the space he needed to clear his mind and distance himself emotionally from the situation.

With Sarthak by his side, Nahar began to rediscover the joy of the trek. The mountains became his escape, the bond with Sarthak his comfort, and the journey his way of regaining control over his emotions. He knew he had a long way to go before he could fully process everything, but for now, he was taking it one step at a time.

And as he looked out over the horizon, surrounded by the vast beauty of the mountains, Nahar felt a small sense of peace. This was his moment. No one could take that away from him.

The next morning, after packing their bags and preparing themselves mentally for the journey ahead, Nahar, Sarthak, Adesh, and Milli made their way to the bus stop. The energy was buzzing with excitement as other trekkers gathered, their backpacks slung over their shoulders, ready for the adventure to Rudra Nath. The bus that would take them to the starting point of the trek arrived shortly, a large vehicle painted with vibrant colours, emblazoned with the name of the trekking company.

Nahar noticed there were about 20 people in total, a relatively small and intimate group, which made the experience feel more personal. He could sense the camaraderie already starting to form among the trekkers, as they exchanged introductions and stories. But for Nahar, his focus was elsewhere.

Knowing what he knew now about Adesh and Milli's interactions, the dynamics between them had shifted dramatically in his mind. The closeness between Adesh and Milli made him uncomfortable, even though he tried to maintain a sense of composure. He didn't want to make a scene or let them see how much it was bothering him, so he calmly kept his distance.

When they boarded the bus, Nahar deliberately chose a seat next to Sarthak, letting Adesh and Milli settle wherever they wanted to. Sarthak, ever the inspiring force, didn't pry into Nahar's decision but gave him a knowing look of understanding. He seemed to have picked up on the tension in the group but respected Nahar's space and privacy.

As the bus pulled out of the station and began winding through the roads that would lead them to the base of the trek, Nahar felt a sense of relief. Sarthak's presence was an advantageous impact—his jovial conversations kept Nahar grounded, distracted from the thoughts gnawing at him. They talked about the trek ahead, their plans for the future, and the beautiful scenery passing by. Sarthak had a natural ability to make anyone feel at ease, and Nahar appreciated his company more than ever.

Every so often, Nahar glanced at the back of the bus where Milli and Adesh sat. They were talking quietly among themselves, and though it made his stomach churn, he reminded himself of his decision: to enjoy this trek, to not let their actions ruin his experience. It was easier said than done, but with Sarthak by his side and the majestic mountains looming in the distance, Nahar found moments of calm.

Chapter 27

Sankri

The bus ride was long, but the group's energy high. The trekkers shared snacks, exchanged travel stories, and started to bond. Some were seasoned hikers, while others, like Nahar, were embarking on their first major trek. It was exciting, and despite the emotional turmoil, Nahar couldn't deny the thrill of what lay ahead.

The bus stopped periodically, allowing the group to stretch their legs and take in the stunning views of the surrounding mountains. Each stop was like a breath of fresh air for Nahar, who used these breaks to further distance himself from the emotional baggage that weighed him down. He and Sarthak would joke around, take photos, and talk with some of the other trekkers, all while subtly avoiding any interaction with Adesh and Milli.

As the bus approached the starting point of the trek, the excitement in the group intensified. The road narrowed, winding higher into the mountains, and the landscape became more rugged. It was a reminder that the adventure was just beginning.

Nahar leaned back on his seat, closing his eyes for a moment, taking in the mountain air, and silently reaffirming his resolve. This was about him now. Whatever happened with Milli and Adesh, whatever tension existed between them, he was determined not to let it govern or prescribe his experience. The trek was his. And he would enjoy every moment of it.

As evening fell, the group reached the picturesque village of Sankri, nestled at the foothills of the majestic mountains. The scenery was eye-opening, with misty clouds wrapping around the towering peaks, and the golden light of the setting sun casting a magical glow over the entire landscape. It almost seemed unreal, like something out of a dream or a painting—the kind of beauty that feels too perfect to exist in reality.

The village itself was charming, the last spot where trekkers could find any of their daily needs before embarking on the more rugged part of the journey. Sankri had a serene vibe, with small,

wooden houses scattered around, smoke rising from chimneys as locals prepared for the evening. The air was crisp and fresh, filled with the scent of pine and earth, which invigorated Nahar's senses.

After the long bus ride, the group was ready to relax for a bit. The trek leader, Sikandar, a seasoned mountain guide with years of experience, directed them to the rooms that had been arranged for their stay. Nahar, Sarthak, Milli, and Adesh dropped their bags in their assigned room, grateful for a moment to rest. Despite the emotional strain from the previous night, Nahar couldn't help but be captivated by the beauty around him. For a brief moment, all of his worries seemed small in the grandness of nature.

Once everyone was settled, Sikandar called the group together for evening snacks. The food was simple but warm and comforting, consisting of local delicacies like aloo paratha and chai. Everyone sat in a circle, enjoying the meal and the camaraderie. There was a sense of excitement buzzing through the group as they chatted about the upcoming trek, exchanged travel stories, and marvelled at the beauty of the place.

After the snacks, Sikandar gathered everyone for an important briefing about the trek ahead. He stood tall, his weathered face showing the wisdom of someone who had spent years in the mountains.

"Welcome to Rudra Nath," he began, his voice strong yet calm, "One of the most beautiful treks in the Himalayas, but also one that demands respect. This journey will test your endurance, both physically and mentally, but trust me—it's worth every step."

He proceeded to give them an overview of the trek, pointing out the key landmarks and challenges they would face. Rudra Nath Peak, known for its stunning views and spiritual significance, was not just a physical challenge but also a spiritual journey for many.

Sikandar's words resonated with Nahar, who was looking for more than just an adventure—he wanted clarity, a sense of purpose. The mountains had a way of offering that to those who were open to the experience. As Sikandar spoke, Nahar felt a flourishing determination within him. He had made a promise to himself not to let the turmoil between him, Milli, and Adesh ruin this experience. This trek would be about him, about finding something deeper within himself.

Sikandar then moved on to the important safety details. He emphasized the importance of staying hydrated, pacing themselves, and being mindful of the altitude. "Listen to your body," he said, "The mountains are unpredictable, and it's crucial to respect them. If you feel unwell, let someone know immediately. This isn't a race-it's a journey."

He also shared some personal advice from his years of guiding trekkers. "The best thing you can bring on this trek is a calm mind. The mountains have their own rhythm—don't try to rush it. Take it slow, enjoy every moment, and let the beauty of the journey sink in."

The group listened intently, some jotting down notes, while others simply soaked in the words. There was a collective feeling of anticipation-the adventure was about to begin.

As the briefing concluded, Sikandar told them to rest well that night because the trek would start early the next morning. Everyone dispersed to their rooms, excited but also slightly nervous about what lay ahead.

Nahar and Sarthak walked back to their room together, exchanging thoughts about the trek. Nahar could sense that Sarthak was just as excited as he was, and they joked about the adventure waiting for them. It felt good to have someone like Sarthak by his side, especially with everything else going on in his life.

That night, as Nahar lay on his bed, staring at the ceiling, he felt a mix of emotions. The mountains had a way of putting things into perspective. Whatever he was feeling about Milli and Adesh seemed small compared to the vastness of the journey ahead. He told himself that this trek would help him find the answers he needed—or at least, some peace.

The silence of the mountains outside lulled him to sleep, preparing him for the adventure that awaited at dawn.

In the dead of night, around 4 AM, Nahar woke up with a heavy feeling pressing down on his chest.

The quiet room was filled with the soft breathing of his companions, but something inside him felt unsettled. He couldn't shake the strange discomfort in his mind, the emotions he had been holding back rising to the surface.

He quietly slipped out of bed, trying not to wake anyone, but Sarthak stirred, noticing Nahar's movements. "Where are you going, man?" Sarthak asked groggily, sensing that something wasn't right.

Nahar, already half-dressed, shrugged into his jacket and whispered back, "I just need some fresh air. I'll be back soon."

Sarthak, still exhausted from the long journey, wanted to join him, concerned about Nahar being out alone in an unacquainted place. "Let me come with you," he said, starting to sit up, but Nahar gently stopped him.

"You're tired, man. Rest up. I just need a few minutes to clear my head. Don't worry, I'll be fine," Nahar reassured him with a small, forced smile.

Sarthak reluctantly nodded and lay back down, his body too fatigued to argue further. "Alright, but don't stay out too long. It's freezing out there," he mumbled before drifting off again.

Nahar zipped up his jacket, pulled on a hat, and quietly opened the door. The cold night air hit him immediately as he stepped outside. The village of Sankri was cloaked in a deep silence, with only the faint rustling of the wind in the trees and the distant sounds of the mountains as his companions. The sky was pitch black, dotted with millions of stars, the moon casting a soft glow over the rugged landscape. It was serene, but inside Nahar's mind, there was a storm brewing.

He walked aimlessly through the village, the cold biting his face, his breath forming small clouds in the air. His thoughts kept circling back to Milli and Adesh. The scene from the previous night was burning into his mind, and no matter how hard he tried to push it away, it kept resurfacing. How could Milli—someone he loved deeply—be so casual, so unfazed, apathetic by what had happened? And Adesh, his friend, crossing a line that could never be.

As Nahar wandered through the forsaken roads, he felt a deep loneliness settling in. He had always known something was off in his relationship with Milli, but seeing it so clearly had shaken him to his core. He had given so much of himself to this relationship, and now, it all felt like it was slipping away. The cold night seemed to mirror the coldness growing in his heart.

His footsteps echoed as he passed by small, shuttered shops and homes, his mind racing with thoughts of betrayal and heartbreak. How had things gone so wrong? He had tried so hard to make this work, even agreeing to this trek in hopes of fixing things, but now, he wasn't sure there was anything left to fix.

He stopped at the edge of the village, where the lights faded, and the vast mountains stretched out before him. He looked up at the stars, their distant light offering little comfort. The mountains, usually a place of peace and clarity, now seemed cold and indifferent to his pain.

Nahar stood there for a while, letting the cold seep into his bones, hoping it would numb the ache in his heart. He wished he could talk to someone, anyone who could understand what he was going through. He thought calling Ruhi again, but it was too late-or too early-for that. He didn't want to burden her with more of his problems.

After what felt like hours, but was only minutes, Nahar turned back towards the village. His hands were numb from the cold, and his heart felt heavy with the weight of everything that had happened. He knew he couldn't avoid this forever. Tomorrow, he would have to face Milli and Adesh again, and the thought of it made his stomach turn.

As he walked back towards the hotel, he made a silent decision. He couldn't let this ruin the trek, as Ruhi had reminded him. This journey was meant to be something special, something that he had looked forward to for so long. He would focus on the trek, on the mountains, and try to push the pain aside-at least for now.

When Nahar returned to the room, everyone was still asleep. He quietly closed the door behind him and sat on the edge of his bed, staring into the darkness. The room felt suffocating, filled with the presence of the people who had hurt him. He knew things would never be the same, but for now, he had to pretend, at least until the trek was over.

With a deep breath, Nahar lay back down, pulling the blanket over him. His mind raced, but his body was exhausted.

Eventually, the cold and exhaustion pulled him into a restless sleep, filled with dreams of betrayal and the unpardoned mountains that awaited him the next day. The next morning, Nahar woke to the soft glow of the sunrise creeping through the cracks in the window.

He blinked his eyes open, the warmth of the early light washing over him as he sat up in bed. The sight outside was astonishing. The sun was just beginning to rise over the towering mountains, casting long shadows across the valley and painting the sky in hues of gold, pink, and orange. It was one of those moments that reminded him why he had come on this trek.

After getting ready and joining the group for breakfast, Nahar could feel the fresh mountain air filling his lungs, invigorating his senses. Everyone seemed to be in high spirits. The early morning excitement was infectious as they gathered in a circle, listening to their trek leader Sikandar give instructions for the day.

Sikandar, standing tall with a calm and confident demeanour, spoke about the trail ahead, explaining the difficulty level and the importance of pacing themselves. "We'll be heading to the first campsite today," he said. "The trek will be tough at times, but don't rush. Enjoy the journey, take in the beauty, and most importantly, help each other." His words were grounding and filled with the wisdom of someone who had done this trek many times before.

Chapter 28

Towards Final Destination

The group set off, the cool morning air still lingering as they marched in a line, the sound of boots crunching against the earth and rocks. Nahar walked next to Sarthak, who had become his closest companion on this trip. They shared occasional conversations, but mostly they admired the raw beauty of the mountains that surrounded them. Milli and Adesh were walking a little ahead, but Nahar had made peace with keeping his distance, focusing on the trek itself and the company of Sarthak.

As they walked, the environment began to shift. The city life they were used to seemed a world away. The towering trees, the pristine streams flowing alongside the trail, and the distant peaks made everything feel surreal. Nature here was untouched, a stark contrast to the urban chaos they had all left behind.

They stopped at several points to rest, and at each spot, the group would take pictures, capturing the stunning scenery and the moments of triumph. Lush green meadows opened up in between dense forests, giving them places to sit, drink water, and catch their breath. The altitude made it tougher to walk, and some of the trekkers began to feel the strain, but they all kept encouraging each other. Nahar, though physically tired, felt mentally refreshed by the peace that the mountains brought him.

At one rest stop, they found a clearing with a perfect view of the valley below. The sun was now higher in the sky, lighting up the distant peaks and casting a beautiful glow over everything. The group sat there for a while, quietly taking in the view. Nahar, though still emotionally recovering, couldn't help but feel grateful for this moment. It was as if nature itself was offering him a chance to heal.

The journey to the first campsite continued, the terrain becoming steeper at times, but the group remained in high spirits, laughing, chatting, and supporting each other.

They passed through small streams, navigated rocky paths, and saw wildflowers blooming in bright colours along the trail. Every now and then, they would stop to take a picture or simply breathe in the fresh mountain air, feeling a deep connection with the land around them.

As they neared their first campsite, Nahar looked around at the people with him. Despite everything that had happened, he knew this trek was an opportunity to rediscover parts of himself that he had lost in the chaos of the relationship. He wasn't there yet, but the mountains were starting to show him the way.

After what felt like an eternity of climbing, Nahar finally spotted the campsite in the distance. The sight gave him a surge of energy, pushing aside the exhaustion that had been weighing on him for the past few hours. His legs ached, his muscles burned, but the moment he saw those brightly coloured tents nestled among the trees, he turned to Sarthak with a reinvigorated spirit.

"Come on, Sarthak, we're almost there!" Nahar called, his voice filled with relief and anticipation. Sarthak, equally tired, smiled and nodded, his pace quickening despite the fatigue.

After 6-7 hours of trekking through challenging terrain, the campsite was a welcome sight. The sun was starting to dip behind the mountains, casting long shadows over the trail, and the cool mountain breeze was a refreshing contrast to the day's heat. Their exhaustion seemed to melt away as they got closer, spurred on by the idea of finally resting.

When they reached the campsite, Nahar and Sarthak collapsed onto the grass, using their trekking bags as makeshift pillows. The relief of lying down was indescribable, and for a few minutes, they simply lay there, looking up at the sky, letting their tired bodies relax.

"This feels like heaven," Sarthak muttered, his eyes half-closed as he caught his breath.

Nahar nodded in agreement, too tired to respond with words. The cool air, the rustle of the leaves, and the distant sound of a stream created an atmosphere of peace, a stark contrast to the gruelling trek they had just completed. Nahar felt a deep sense of accomplishment. Despite everything going on in his personal life, he had made it here, and the mountains seemed to reward him with this serene moment of rest.

After a while, other trekkers began arriving at the campsite. One by one, people trickled in, just as tired but equally relieved. They all gathered around, sitting on the grass in small groups, chatting quietly or simply resting in silence. There was a shared sense of accomplishment among them — they had made it through the first day of the trek, and now they could finally take a break.

Milli and Adesh arrived shortly after, joining the rest of the group. Nahar noticed them out of the corner of his eye but chose to focus on the moment of peace he had created for himself. He wasn't ready to let the situation with them affect his mood, especially after the effort it had taken to reach this point.

The trekkers were all waiting for Sikandar, the trek leader, to give them the next set of instructions. Until then, everyone settled into the grassy clearing, sharing snacks, water, and stories from the day's journey. Nahar, feeling the warmth of solidarity among the group, sat quietly, letting the exhaustion of the day slowly fade as the cool mountain air refreshed his mind.

Looking around at the peaceful scenery, Nahar felt some kind of shift within him. The trek was about more than just the physical journey; it was becoming a mental and emotional one, a chance for him to find clarity amid the chaos that had been weighing him down. Sitting there, surrounded by nature and people who were just as worn out but happy, he realized this was the escape he needed.

For the first time in a while, Nahar felt a sliver of hope - maybe this trek would be the beginning of something new, a chance to heal.

As everyone settled in at the campsite, Sikandar, the trek leader, arrived and began the process of tent allotment. His voice carried across the clearing as he called out names and assigned tents based on gender, following the usual trek norms. It was the expected setup-girls in one tent, boys in others-providing a sense of comfort and routine for Nahar, who welcomed the idea of space from the complex dynamics of the group.

Just as Sikandar was about to allot the tents, Milli raised her hand, stepping forward and interrupting the process.

"Actually, Sikandar," she said confidently, "we four—me, Nahar, Adesh, and Sarthak—will share one tent."

The statement caught Nahar completely off guard. She hadn't consulted him or Sarthak about this arrangement, and he could feel a knot forming in his stomach. He glanced at Sarthak, who looked equally surprised but remained silent, not wanting to create a scene.

Sikandar paused, looking between the group members with a raised eyebrow. "Are you sure?" he asked, clearly accustomed to more traditional tent arrangements. "Typically, I'd keep the girls together and boys in separate tents. It's more comfortable that way."

Milli smiled, her tone casual and insistent. "Yes, we've been traveling together, and we're fine sharing one tent."

Nahar felt a wave of disappointment wash over him. Deep down, he knew this wasn't right- ethically or emotionally. He had been looking forward to having some space, especially after the events of the past night. The idea of spending the next three nights in such close quarters with Milli and Adesh, after everything he had observed, was suffocating. He felt trapped in a situation that only deepened his frustration.

But, as always, Nahar didn't say anything. He kept his thoughts to himself, bottling up the discomfort that had been growing since the trek began. He didn't want to cause a scene or create more tension, especially with Sarthak and Sikandar present. It wasn't in his nature to object openly, even when his emotions were screaming otherwise.

Sikandar, sensing no objection from the rest of the group, shrugged and said, "Alright, if that's what you all want, I'll allot the tent to the four of you."

Nahar gave a subtle sigh but said nothing, his mind racing with conflicting thoughts. He couldn't understand why Milli had made the decision without consulting him. It felt like a disregard for his feelings, and now, he had no choice but to endure the awkwardness for the rest of the trek.

The group grabbed their bags and headed towards the tent that had been allotted to them. Nahar carried his things silently, his mind buzzing with disappointment and frustration. He could feel the emotional weight of the situation bearing down on him as he followed the others into the tent.

Once inside, they all placed their bags down, with Milli settling in comfortably, as if nothing was out of the ordinary. Nahar, on the other hand, felt an overwhelming sense of unease. This wasn't how he had imagined the trek, and now, the thought of spending the next few nights in such a tight space, with unresolved feelings simmering beneath the surface, was unbearable.

As he watched Milli chat with Adesh and Sarthak, Nahar quietly withdrew into his thoughts, realizing that the situation wasn't just about the tent. It symbolized the larger issues in their relationship the lack of communication, Milli's disregard for his feelings, and the widening gap between what they wanted from each other.

For now, though, all he could do was try to hold himself together, hoping that the beauty of the mountains would help distract him from the storm brewing inside. He knew these next few days would be a test, not just physically but emotionally as well.

After some rest, Sikandar announced that there would be a short trek to a nearby frozen lake. It was optional, allowing those who were too tired to stay back at the camp and relax. Nahar, eager to immerse himself in the natural beauty and distract his mind from everything that had been weighing him down, decided to join the hike. Sarthak, however, looked exhausted and complained of a headache probably due to dehydration and the altitude. He opted to stay back and rest in the tent.

"I'll be fine here," Sarthak reassured Nahar. "You go ahead and enjoy the lake."

Nahar nodded, slightly disappointed that his closest companion on this trek wouldn't be joining him. He grabbed his gear, put on a warm jacket, and headed out to join the others, who were already gathering near the camp. Milli and Adesh were standing together, but Nahar distanced himself from them, choosing instead to mingle with the other trekkers he hadn't interacted with, much before.

As the group started hiking toward the lake, Nahar found himself surrounded by new faces, many of whom were enthusiastic and eager to explore the beauty of the mountains. The path to the lake was serene, with snow-covered terrain and patches of frozen ground glittering under the afternoon sun. With every step, Nahar felt a little lighter, the stunning scenery momentarily pulling him away from the emotional turmoil he had been experiencing.

On the way, he struck up a conversation with a fellow trekker named Arjun, who was from a nearby town and shared Nahar's love for nature. They bonded over their mutual excitement for the trek, the surreal landscapes around them, and their plans for future adventures. This interaction felt refreshing for Nahar it was an escape from the tension within his group and Arjun's company provided an opportunity to simply enjoy the experience without emotional baggage.

As they reached the frozen lake, the group marvelled at its beauty. The lake, encased in ice, reflected the surrounding mountains and the pale blue sky above, creating a pleasingly beautiful sight. The air was crisp, and there was a peaceful stillness to the place, as if time had slowed down. Nahar, standing at the edge of the frozen lake, felt a moment of pure tranquillity, something he hadn't experienced in a while.

While some trekkers took photos and admired the scenery, Nahar took a quiet moment for himself, breathing deeply and absorbing the grandeur of the landscape. The sight of the frozen lake, the towering peaks, and the wide-open sky made his problems seem small and insignificant. For a few moments, he felt connected to the world in a way that he hadn't in a long time.

As the sun began to dip behind the mountains, casting a golden glow over the ice, the group began to head back to the camp. Nahar found himself laughing and joking with the others, enjoying the fellowship that came naturally in the shared experience of the trek.

By the time they returned to camp, Nahar was in much better spirits, having made new connections and shared memorable moments at the frozen lake. Though he knew the underlying issues with Milli and Adesh were still present, the trek reminded him that there were beautiful experiences and meaningful relationships beyond the tangled emotions he had been dealing with.

For now, he felt a newfound sense of determination to focus on the trek and enjoy the remaining days, especially with Sarthak by his side. The mountains offered a sense of clarity, and Nahar was beginning to realize that the trek, in many ways, was helping him understand himself better.

On the way back to the camp from the frozen lake, Nahar found himself walking alongside Sikandar, the trek leader. Sikandar had been a quiet but authoritative presence throughout the journey so far, guiding the group with confidence. Seeing an opportunity to learn more about the mountains and perhaps distract himself further, Nahar struck up a conversation with him.

"You must have seen a lot in these mountains," Nahar said, his curiosity piqued. "What's the most memorable experience you've had on a trek?"

Sikandar smiled, the kind that hinted at untold stories. "Oh, I've had my fair share of adventures out here. Some of them are thrilling, and others are... unsettling, to say the least."

Nahar's interest was immediately sparked. "Unsettling? What do you mean?"

Sikandar's expression grew more serious as they continued walking along the snow-dusted path. "These mountains are beautiful, but they can also be dangerous, unpredictable. I've had a few close calls over the years, and some of the things I've seen—well, they can make you question what's real."

Seeing the excitement on Nahar's face, Sikandar began sharing one of his most eerie experiences. "There was this one time, a few years ago," he began, his voice lowering as though the memory itself was enough to summon the shadows of the past. "We were leading a small group to a similar campsite near Rudra Nath. It was the end of the day, like today, and the sun had already set. We were setting up our tents when one of the trekkers noticed something odd—a figure standing near the tree line, just beyond the camp."

Nahar leaned in closer, listening intently. The air around them seemed to grow colder.

"At first, we thought it was someone from the village, maybe a local," Sikandar continued. "But the figure didn't move. It just stood there, barely visible in the fading light. One of the trekkers waved at it, but there was no response. A couple of us went closer to see if the person needed help, but as we got nearer, the figure seemed to dissolve into the trees, as if it had never been there."

Nahar shivered, though he wasn't sure if it was from the cold or the story.

"Later that night, some of the trekkers swore they heard whispers coming from the same direction, though none of us could find anything. The locals, when we asked them the next morning, said it wasn't unusual. They believe that the spirits of those who died on these trails sometimes linger, especially when there's been a recent avalanche or accident."

Sikandar paused for a moment, letting the story sink in.

Nahar's mind raced as he imagined the scene. "Did you ever figure out what it was?" he asked, his voice hushed.

Sikandar shook his head. "No. And that's the thing about these mountains—they don't always give you answers. Sometimes, you're left with only the questions."

As they continued walking, Sikandar shared more stories, some thrilling and some haunting. There were tales of close encounters with wildlife, sudden changes in weather that left trekkers stranded, and even one about a fellow guide who had once disappeared for an entire night, only to return the next morning with no memory of where he had been.

By the time they neared the camp, Nahar was both thrilled and unsettled. The beauty of the mountains had always been apparent, but now he understood that there was a mysterious, almost mystical side to them as well. The stories had ignited something in him—a deeper respect for the wilderness, but also a sense of awe at the unknown forces that might be at play in such remote places.

As the camp came into view, with the warm glow of the fire and the familiar faces of the trekkers, Nahar felt a strange mix of emotions. On one hand, the mountains seemed more dangerous than ever, but on the other, they also felt more alive, filled with secrets waiting to be uncovered.

As Nahar returned to the tent after dinner, his heart felt heavy. The excitement of the trek and the beauty of the mountains could only momentarily distract him from the storm brewing inside. The thought of sharing the tent with Milli and Adesh gnawed at him, making it impossible to relax. The arrangement felt wrong, and as the others busied themselves with their sleeping bags, Nahar quietly struggled with his emotions.

When they finally entered the tent, Milli chose the corner spot, which was close to Adesh. She spread out her belongings with ease, not showing the slightest discomfort. Nahar, trying to hide his unease, laid his sleeping bag beside Sarthak, who had already started drifting off to sleep from exhaustion. Adesh settled into the spot next to Milli without hesitation, the two of them lying so close that it unsettled Nahar deeply.

As he lay in his sleeping bag, Nahar's mind was racing. His thoughts bounced from one memory to another, each one intensifying the hurt. The betrayal he felt had started to manifest physically, his chest tightening, his stomach knotting with unease. How could things have spiralled to this point? he wondered. How could Milli be so indifferent, so casual, after all they'd been through? She was sleeping next to Adesh as if it were the most normal thing in the world, as though Nahar didn't exist.

In the dim light of the tent, Nahar glanced at Milli. Her eyes were already closed, her breathing steady. She looked peaceful, unaffected by the emotional turmoil that Nahar was drowning in. The realization that she didn't even seem to care cut him deeper than he had anticipated. How could she not feel the tension? How could she sleep so soundly knowing how fragile their relationship had become?

Adesh, too, appeared comfortable, his presence next to Milli causing an unspoken rift between him and Nahar. The two of them were supposed to be his closest companions, yet now they felt like strangers. The sense of betrayal was overwhelming. For Nahar, this wasn't just about sharing a tent-it was symbolic of something far deeper, the erosion of trust and emotional connection that once existed between them.

As Nahar lay there, he couldn't stop thinking about the many moments he had shared with Milli- how much he had opened his heart to her, how vulnerable he had been. He had trusted her, believed in their connection, only to now feel betrayed by her coldness. She hadn't even acknowledged the sleeping arrangements, nor had she seemed to care about how uncomfortable he might feel.

Nahar tried to distract himself by staring at the tent's roof, but the sound of Milli's quiet breathing and the closeness between her and Adesh was impossible to ignore. How had things gone so wrong? He turned to face the other side of the tent, trying to block them from his view, but it didn't help. The pain, the sense of betrayal, and the loneliness only grew.

Every small movement in the tent seemed amplified. When Adesh shifted slightly in his sleeping bag, Nahar caught a glimpse of his hand resting casually near Milli's stomach. A surge of emotion flooded Nahar's mind- anger, disappointment, disbelief. This was the final straw. Nahar couldn't take it anymore. It was one thing for Milli to be distant, but for Adesh to act so intimately around her, knowing full well the history between Nahar and Milli, was devastating.

His heart felt like it was shattering as he watched them. He couldn't decide what dis hurt him more? The fact that Milli seemed so unaffected, or the fact that Adesh, his best friend, didn't seem to care about how his actions were impacting him. The reality of the situation was finally sinking in, and it hit Nahar hard. He had lost them both, not just as a romantic partner and a friend, but as people he could trust.

The weight of the situation pressed down on him, making it impossible to stay in the tent any longer. The air felt thick, suffocating, and Nahar knew he needed to get out before he broke down completely in front of them. He couldn't bear the thought of showing his vulnerability to people who no longer seemed to care. Silently, he slipped out of his sleeping bag and quietly left the tent, careful not to wake anyone.

The cold night air hit his face as he stepped outside, but it was a relief compared to the emotional suffocation he had felt inside. He took a few deep breaths, trying to calm the storm inside him, but it wasn't working. The pain was too intense, too raw. His thoughts were racing uncontrollably—the betrayal, the loss, the realization that the people he loved most had changed beyond recognition.

He walked away from the camp, heading toward the edge of the mountainside. The view was so peaceful, calm, composed. The moon casting a soft glow on the snow-capped peaks, but Nahar couldn't appreciate it. All he could think about was how everything in his life seemed to be crumbling apart. Tears began to stream down his face, though he tried to stop them.

For a long while, Nahar stood there alone, his heart heavy and broken, trying to come to terms with the harsh reality of his situation. The bond he once cherished was now nothing more than a painful memory. He had trusted Milli with everything, and now she had drifted away, not only from him but from the relationship they had worked so hard to build. Adesh's betrayal only made it worse, as it was a double blow to his heart.

Eventually, Nahar wiped his tears and returned to the camp. As he re-entered the tent, he felt a deep sense of resolve. This trek wouldn't be ruined by what had happened. He would no longer let Milli or Adesh's actions destroy his spirit. He would find strength within himself, even if it meant detaching from them emotionally. He knew things would never be the same, but at that moment, he decided to focus on himself and make the most of the trek.

Chapter 29

Fresh Resilience

The next morning, Nahar woke up feeling the weight of exhaustion, both physically and emotionally. His body was sore from the long hike and restless sleep, but his mind felt even heavier from the events of the previous night. As he sat up, he could see the others beginning to stir, the cold mountain air filling the tent. Sarthak, always a light sleeper, was already up and stretching, while Adesh and Milli were still wrapped in their sleeping bags, oblivious to Nahar's inner turmoil.

Nahar decided to focus on the present and stepped outside the tent to start his morning. The air was crisp and biting, but the view around him was mesmerizing. The sun had just begun to rise, casting a golden hue over the snow-covered peaks. For a brief moment, the beauty of the mountains provided him with some solace, as if nature itself was trying to soothe his wounded heart.

As he made his way to the makeshift kitchen area, one of the trek staff handed him a cup of black tea and a small packet of cookies. The warmth of the tea was comforting against the chill, and he found a spot near a rock to sip it in peace, gazing out at the mountains. For a while, he allowed himself to just be, trying to absorb the beauty of his surroundings, hoping it would give him the strength he needed for the day ahead.

After finishing his tea, Nahar joined the rest of the group for breakfast. The atmosphere was lively, with people discussing the trek and sharing their excitement for the next leg of the journey. Nahar tried to blend in, keeping his mood light despite the heaviness in his heart. As he ate, the warm food gave him a bit of energy, and he focused on staying present, trying not to let his thoughts wander back to the night before.

When breakfast was over, it was time to wash up. Nahar went to the handwash station, a simple setup with a basin and some cold water stored in large containers. He approached the basin, dipped his hands into the water, and immediately recoiled. The water was ice-cold, colder than anything he had expected. A sharp chill shot through his fingers, and for a second, he couldn't imagine how people were managing to use it.

"This water is freezing!" Nahar exclaimed quietly, shaking his hands to get rid of the cold. It felt as if his fingers had gone numb the moment they touched the water. He glanced around, noticing that others were having the same reaction, laughing and shivering as they tried to quickly wash up and escape the biting cold.

Despite the freezing water, Nahar managed to wash up, but it made him realize just how different life was up here in the mountains. Everything was harsh yet more beautiful, yes, but also more challenging. The cold, the exhaustion, the isolation—all of it combined to create a unique experience, one that was testing him in every way possible.

As he dried his hands, Nahar looked back at the tent where the others were finishing up breakfast. Sarthak caught his eye and gave him a knowing smile, as if sensing that Nahar was still processing everything. Sarthak's presence felt like an anchor, a reminder that despite the emotional storm he was going through, there were still people in his life who cared.

The second day of the trek was one of the discoveries and deepening within the bonds. Nahar, Sarthak, Milli, and Adesh started the morning with new energy, despite the physical demands of the journey. The early hours were filled with glorified views as they made their way up the rugged path, the landscape changing from dense forests to rocky trails. Nahar found himself enjoying the company of Sarthak more and more; their shared sense of humour and mutual understanding made the trek lighter, even as the path grew steeper.

As the group trekked onward, Sikandar, the trek leader, kept everyone engaged with stories from his many years of experience in the mountains. Nahar was particularly interested in these tales, some of which were thrilling and even a bit eerie. These stories served as a distraction from his inner turmoil about Milli and the situation in their shared tent.

When they finally reached the second campsite, nestled amidst towering peaks, the exhaustion was palpable. But their spirits were quickly lifted when they spotted a small, rustic shop near the camp. The shop, with its humble offerings of momos and Maggi, became the highlight of the day. The cold mountain air and the physical exertion had heightened everyone's appetite, and the idea of tasting "pahadi" Maggi and momos added a layer of excitement to the day.

As they gathered at the shop, huddled together in the cool afternoon, the group eagerly ordered their meals. The warmth of the freshly cooked food contrasted sharply with the chilly air, making each bite feel like a small comfort. The momos were perfectly steamed, and the Maggi, with its simple yet savoury flavours, was a welcome treat. For a moment, all the tension seemed to melt away as they shared this meal, laughing and chatting like old friends. Even Milli seemed more relaxed, and for a while, the awkwardness between her, Adesh, and Nahar faded into the background.

After lunch, with their stomachs full and their bodies weary, they returned to the tents for a much-needed rest. Nahar, lying on his back in the tent, reflected on the day. Despite the unease that still lingered, especially with Milli and Adesh sharing the same space, he found solace in the simplicity of the day's events. The laughter, the shared stories, and the taste of the local food created a sense of normalcy that he desperately needed.

Yet, as he closed his eyes to rest, Nahar couldn't completely shake off the thoughts that had been haunting him since the previous night. He knew the trek was only just beginning, and the challenges ahead weren't just physical. Still, he allowed himself to drift into sleep, hoping that tomorrow would bring more moments of peace like those he experienced today.

The day had been a mix of highs and lows, but Nahar was starting to see the value in focusing on the positives-the friendships, the beauty of the mountains, and the small joys that came with this journey. Even as he rested, he felt a subtle shift within himself, an understanding that while he couldn't control everything, he could choose to find solace in the good moments and the people who truly cared about him, like Sarthak. This newfound clarity was perhaps the first step towards healing, even amidst the ongoing complexities of his relationship with Milli.

As the evening set in, the atmosphere around the camp became lively. Everyone, including Nahar, Sarthak, Milli, Adesh, and others, gathered outside their tents, sitting on the cool grass and enjoying the crisp mountain air. Laughter and light-hearted conversations filled the air as they shared stories and experiences from the trek so far.

Sikandar, the trek leader, soon approached the group, carrying a bundle of gear. He handed out special snow shoes to each person, explaining that the terrain ahead would be covered in snow, and these shoes would make the walk easier. His voice carried a mix of authority and excitement as he informed them of the plan for the next day. "We will start the final ascent at 3 AM," he announced. "The goal is to reach the peak of Rudra Nath by sunrise. It's going to be challenging, but the view will be worth every step."

The idea of trekking through snow in the early hours of the morning sent a thrill through the group, but it also brought a sense of seriousness. Sikandar advised them all to get as much rest as possible that night. The thought of witnessing the sunrise from the peak of Rudra Nath was a powerful motivator, and everyone nodded in agreement.

As the evening wore on, Nahar found himself quietly observing the dynamics around him. The bond with

Sarthak had grown stronger, and he felt a sense of comfort in his company. However, the lingering discomfort of sharing a tent with Milli and Adesh still gnawed at him. Despite the brotherhood and the surreal environment, Nahar couldn't shake off the unsettling feelings that had been building up since the start of the trek.

The group slowly dispersed to their tents as the night deepened. Nahar, mentally preparing himself for the early start, adjusted his sleeping bag beside Sarthak, making sure to keep some distance from Milli and Adesh. His mind raced as he tried to calm himself for the challenging day ahead.

But as he lay there, under the vast starry sky, the anticipation of the upcoming trek mixed with the emotional turmoil he was trying to suppress. The cold mountain air did little to soothe his troubled thoughts, but he knew he had to focus on the journey ahead. Tomorrow would be a test not just of his physical endurance, but of his emotional resilience as well.

Eventually, the exhaustion of the day took over, and Nahar drifted into a restless sleep, his mind heavy with the conflicting emotions he had been battling throughout the trek.

The night was still and the air was crisp as Nahar and the rest of the group slowly woke up at 2 a.m. The cold mountain air felt sharp against their skin as they emerged from their tents, groggy but filled with a quiet anticipation. The camp was a hive of subdued activity, with everyone preparing for the most challenging part of their trek. The glow from headlamps and the distant twinkle of stars provided the only light in the otherwise pitch-black surroundings.

After quickly freshening up, they gathered around the small mess tent where a simple breakfast had been prepared-something light to fuel them for the gruelling climb ahead. The group ate in near silence, each person focused on the task ahead. There was a palpable sense of excitement in the air, mingled with a hint of nervousness. Nahar could feel his heartbeat quicken with a mix of anticipation and adrenaline. By 3a.m. they were all geared up, looking like a team of mountaineers ready for a major expedition. Their boots were laced tightly, and their snowshoes were secured, essential for the snow-covered paths they would soon encounter. The headlamps created small beams of light that pierced the darkness, illuminating the trail just enough to see where they were stepping.

Sikandar, the ever-reliable leader, gave them one final round of instructions. His voice was steady, filled with the experience of countless treks like this one. "Stay close together, and watch your footing. The path is narrow in some places, and it's easy to slip. But remember, it's not a race. Pace yourself, and look out for each other," he said, his words a mix of caution and encouragement.

With a final nod from Sikandar, the group set off, moving in a single file through the darkness. The only sounds were the crunch of their boots on the snow and the rhythmic breathing of the trekkers. The trail was steep and winding, and the cold air grew sharper as they ascended, biting into their exposed skin. But the thought of reaching the summit in time to see the sunrise kept them moving, one determined step after another.

Chapter 30

Peak: Fragility of Forever

As they climbed higher, Nahar's thoughts wandered to the events of the past few days. The emotional strain he had been under-weighed heavily on him, but the challenge of the trek gave him a welcome distraction. Each step forward felt like a small victory, a way to push through the confusion and hurt that had clouded his mind.

The group trudged on through the snow, the darkness slowly beginning to lighten as the first hints of dawn approached. The anticipation built with every step, knowing that soon they would be at the peak, witnessing a sunrise that few ever get to see. Despite the physical strain, Nahar felt a surge of energy, fuelled by the beauty and intensity of the moment.

As Nahar and the group continued their midnight trek to the Rudra Nath peak, the excitement they had initially felt began to wane, replaced by the stark reality of the challenge before them. The air was thin, and each breath felt like a laborious effort. The cold was intense, cutting through their layers of clothing and chilling them to the bone. The only sounds were the crunch of snow underfoot and the occasional gust of wind that swept across the mountainside.

The group moved slowly, their progress hampered by the steep incline and the treacherous, snow-covered path. Every step required careful attention, as a single misstep could lead to a fall. Nahar could feel the weight of exhaustion settling into his limbs, but he pushed on, driven by the determination to reach the peak.

After several hours of arduous trekking, when the cold and fatigue seemed almost unbearable, they spotted a small shop nestled in the darkness ahead. It was a beacon of hope in the otherwise unforgiving environment, and the group eagerly made their way towards it.

Entering the shop felt like stepping into a different world. The warmth inside was a stark contrast to the frigid cold outside, and it was an instant relief to their frozen bodies. The small, dimly lit space was filled with the comforting scent of hot tea and snacks. The group quickly found seats, their faces flushed from the cold and the exertion of the trek.

Nahar and his companions ordered hot tea and snacks, and as they sipped the steaming liquid, they could feel warmth spreading through their bodies. The tea, though simple, felt like a luxury in that moment, soothing their throats and lifting their spirits. The snacks provided much-needed energy, and the group chatted lightly, their spirits buoyed by the temporary respite from the cold and exhaustion.

The atmosphere inside the shop was cosy, almost homely. The shopkeeper, a local from the mountains, chatted with them about the trek, offering words of encouragement and advice. Nahar listened intently, appreciating the wisdom of someone who knew these mountains well. The conversation turned to stories of past trekkers, and the shopkeeper shared tales of both success and struggle, each story a reminder of the unpredictability of the mountains.

As they rested, Nahar felt a rekindled friendship with the group. The shared struggle of the trek had bonded them in a way that nothing else could. Even Sarthak, who had been relatively new to the group, felt like an old friend now. There was a silent understanding among them—a recognition of the challenge they were facing together.

After some time, feeling recharged both physically and mentally, the group knew it was time to continue. Reluctantly, they left the warmth of the shop, steeling themselves for the next leg of the journey. The cold outside was sharp, biting at their faces as they stepped back into the night, but they were ready.

With renewed determination, they resumed their trek. The peak still lay ahead, hidden in the darkness, but they were closer now, and the thought of reaching it filled them with a sense of purpose. They moved forward, small steps on the snowy path, each one bringing them closer to their goal. The warmth of the shop lingered in their minds, a memory of comfort in the midst of the harshness of the trek,

As Nahar continued his trek, the first glimpse of the Rudra Nath peak came into view, silhouetted against the dark sky. Though still distant, the sight of the peak filled him with a surge of satisfaction and determination. The peak stood like a silent guardian, a goal that had seemed so far away just hours ago, now within reach.

Despite the darkness that still enveloped the mountains, there was a faint glow on the horizon, hinting at the approaching dawn. The sky above was dotted with stars, and the cold, crisp air seemed to sharpen Nahar's senses. He could see the faint outlines of the other trekkers ahead, around 20 to 30 people making their way up the path. They moved at a steady pace, their breaths visible in the cold air.

In that moment, something shifted in Nahar's mind. A realization dawned over him: he knew he could reach the peak, but what if he pushed himself even harder? What if he became the first to reach the summit? The thought ignited a new fire within him. It was no longer just about reaching the top; it was about leading the way, proving to himself that he could conquer not just the mountain, but his own limitations.

With this newfound resolve, Nahar quickened his pace. His tired legs seemed to find a new reserve of energy, and his footsteps grew more determined. He began to weave through the group ahead of him, carefully navigating the narrow path while conserving his energy for the final push. The cold that had once numbed him now seemed to fuel his determination, and the darkness no longer felt daunting but instead filled him with a sense of purpose.

As he passed other trekkers, some of them looked at him with surprise, their own exhaustion evident on their faces. But Nahar was in a zone, his focus narrowed to the peak ahead. The rhythmic crunch of snow under his boots became a mantra, each step propelling him closer to his goal.

The path grew steeper, the air thinner, but Nahar's resolve only strengthened. He kept his breathing steady, his gaze fixed on the peak that now seemed to beckon him forward. The distance between him and the summit was closing, and with it, a sense of achievement swelled within him. This was his moment, a test of his willpower, and he was determined to emerge victorious.

As he continued to ascend, the sky began to lighten, the first rays of dawn breaking through the darkness. The stars started to fade, replaced by a soft, golden glow on the horizon. Nahar could feel the anticipation building within him, not just for reaching the peak, but for witnessing the sunrise from the top, a reward for all his effort.

With each step, the peak loomed closer, the path becoming steeper and more challenging. But Nahar pressed on, his mind focused on one thing: being the first to stand at the summit. The thought of conquering the mountain, of pushing himself beyond what he had thought possible, drove him forward with unrelenting determination.

Finally, after what felt like an eternity, the summit was just a short distance away. Nahar's heart pounded with excitement and exhaustion, his body aching but his spirit unbroken. He was almost there, the first among the group, ready to claim the peak as his own personal victory.

And then, with one final push, he reached it. Nahar stood at the top of Rudra Nath, the first of the trekkers to do so. The world seemed to pause as he looked out over the vast expanse of mountains and valleys below, the first light of dawn painting the sky in hues of pink and orange. The sense of accomplishment was overwhelming, a mixture of pride, relief, and awe at the beauty that surrounded him.

For a moment, Nahar simply stood there, taking it all in—the majesty of the mountains, the quietude of the early morning, and the knowledge that he had pushed himself beyond his limits to achieve something extraordinary. It was a moment of pure triumph, one that he would carry with him long after the trek was over.

As Nahar reached the peak of Rudra Nath with five others, he was enveloped by the majestic, vibrant, stunning view of the sunrise. The sky was painted in shades of orange and pink, illuminating the snow-capped mountains and casting a golden hue over the landscape. In the midst of this awe-inspiring beauty stood a small temple dedicated to Lord Shiva.

Feeling a rush of gratitude and emotion, Nahar stepped into the temple. He found a quiet corner and sat in a meditative posture, closing his eyes to absorb the moment fully. The chill in the air contrasted sharply with the warmth he felt inside as he focused on his breathing, allowing the tranquillity of the surroundings to wash over him.

Thoughts flooded his mind—memories of the past few months, the ups and downs, and especially the painful moments he had faced. Tears began to flow as he reflected on his journey, remembering the heartache of discovering Milli's changing feelings and the betrayal he felt from Adesh. Yet, amidst the pain, he recognized these experiences as vital parts of his growth.

"Thank you for this beautiful life," he whispered, feeling a deep sense of connection to something greater than himself. He understood that these challenges were not just obstacles, but indicators guiding him towards a better understanding of himself and his desires.

After what felt like an eternity, Nahar opened his eyes, looking around the small temple, now filled with the soft glow of the rising sun. He took a moment to soak in the serenity before standing up, feeling lighter and more resolute. As he exited the temple, he took a deep breath, ready to face whatever came next, knowing that he was on the path to healing.

After Nahar and the small group witnessed the enchanting, serene sunrise at Rudra Nath peak, the rest of the group members gradually made their way to the summit. The excitement and energy were palpable as everyone took in the stunning views. The clear morning sky allowed them to see for miles, with the sun casting a warm glow over the surrounding mountains.

For the next two to three hours, the group enjoyed the serenity and dazzle of the peak, taking countless photos, sharing stories, and simply absorbing the experience. The small temple of Lord Shiva became a focal point for many, with some offering prayers and others finding a moment of peace in its presence.

Eventually, Sikandar, the trek leader, gathered everyone for the descent. Though the group was reluctant to leave, they knew it was time to head back. The journey down was filled with chatter about the sunrise, the views, and the sense of accomplishment that came with reaching the peak.

By the time they reached their campsite, it was well into the afternoon. Exhausted but exhilarated, they all sat down for lunch, sharing their experiences and reliving the highlights of the trek. Nahar, though physically tired, felt a deep sense of fulfilment. The beauty of the peak and the emotional release he had experienced at the temple lingered in his mind.

After lunch, they packed up their belongings and began the trek back to their first campsite. The descent was easier, but the memories of the sunrise kept playing in their minds. As the evening approached and they finally reached the first campsite, the group was quiet, each person lost in their thoughts, replaying the awe-inspiring scenes they had witnessed that morning.

That night, as they settled into their tents, the conversations were more subdued, reflecting the deep impact the trek had on everyone. The image of the sun rising over the mountains, the temple at the peak, and the bond they had all formed during the journey stayed with them, creating a shared memory that they would all cherish for years to come. Nahar, in particular, felt a sense of closure and peace, as if the mountain had helped him begin to heal from the wounds of his recent past.

After the long day of trekking and the emotional high of witnessing the sunrise at Rudra Nath peak, everyone was exhausted. The group returned to their tents to rest, preparing for another night in the mountains. As usual, Nahar settled in on the side of the tent next to Sarthak, with Milli and Adesh on the other sides.

Chapter 31

SARTHAK: Familiar Stranger

Sarthak, who had grown close to Nahar during the trek, couldn't shake the feeling that something was off between Nahar, Milli, and Adesh. He had noticed the subtle tension between them, the way Nahar seemed distant whenever Milli and Adesh were together. Sarthak's intuition told him that there was more going on, but he wasn't sure how or when to bring it up. The close quarters of the tent didn't feel like the right place for such a sensitive conversation, especially with everyone so tired.

As they all settled into their sleeping bags, the only sounds were the rustling of fabric and the occasional gust of wind outside the tent. Despite the physical exhaustion, Nahar's mind was still restless, but he kept his thoughts to himself. Sarthak, lying beside him, could sense the unease but decided to wait for a better moment to ask Nahar about it.

Eventually, the fatigue of the day overtook them, and one by one, they all drifted off to sleep. The night was quiet, the only noise coming from the distant rustle of the trees and the soft murmur of the mountain wind. Despite the underlying tension, the group was bound by the shared experiences of the trek, and sleep offered them a brief respite from their worries and concerns.

The next morning, Nahar and Sarthak woke up simultaneously, the first rays of the sun filtering through the tent's fabric. The air was crisp and cold, a reminder that they were still deep in the mountains. After freshening up, they decided to take a walk around the campsite before the rest of the group stirred.

As they walked along the narrow paths lined with wildflowers and dew-covered grass, Sarthak decided it was time to have a deeper conversation with Nahar. The trek had brought them closer, and he felt comfortable enough to ask about Nahar's plans once the adventure ended.

"So, Nahar, what's on your mind? What are you planning to do after we get back?" Sarthak asked, trying to keep the tone casual.

Nahar, still feeling the weight of everything that had happened with Milli and Adesh, took a moment before responding. "I'm not entirely sure," he said, exhaling deeply. "I've been thinking a lot lately, especially about what comes next. I guess I'll just focus on the next steps in my career, maybe apply for some jobs or start preparing for exams again."

Sarthak nodded, sensing there was more on Nahar's mind. "And what about… everything else?" he ventured, leaving the question open-ended, giving Nahar space to talk about whatever he wanted.

Nahar sighed, glancing at the mountains that surrounded them. "It's complicated," he admitted. "But I'm trying not to let it cloud my mind. This trek has been a good distraction, a way to clear my head."

As they continued their walk, they reached the small shop that had become a familiar spot during their stay. Nahar walked up to the counter and purchased a box of cigarettes, a habit he seldom indulged in but felt drawn to during times of stress. He offered one to Sarthak, who took it, and they both lit up, the smoke curling into the chilly morning air.

They stood there for a while, leaning against the wooden railing outside the shop, the landscape stretching out before them in all its rugged beauty. The conversation drifted back to lighter topics-memories from the trek, shared jokes, and plans for the future.

Nahar felt a small sense of relief. Talking with Sarthak was easier than he had expected, and although he hadn't revealed everything on his mind, just knowing that he had someone to talk to made a difference. They continued their conversation, letting the peacefulness of the morning and the bond they had formed over the past days carry them forward.

As the sun rose higher and the early morning mist began to lift, Sarthak finally felt the moment was right to delve deeper. They had been talking about their plans, about life after the trek, but something was clearly weighing heavily on Nahar. Sarthak decided to ask directly.

"Nahar," Sarthak began carefully, "I've noticed you've been... different lately. I mean, more distant, maybe? And I'm just wondering... how are things with Milli? You don't have to tell me if you don't want to, but if you need someone to listen, I'm here."

Nahar had already finished two cigarettes, the second one just a way to keep his hands busy while his mind raced. He looked exhausted—not just physically, but emotionally drained. The weight of the past few days, combined with everything that had been simmering beneath the surface, was too much to bear in silence any longer.

Taking a deep breath, Nahar finally decided to let it all out. "It's been a mess, Sarthak. A complete mess," he said, his voice heavy with frustration and sadness. "This trek... it was supposed to be something special, a way to maybe find some clarity, but it's just made everything more complicated."

Sarthak remained silent, letting Nahar take his time to gather his thoughts.

Nahar continued, his words spilling out in a rush, "Milli and I... things were going well, or at least I thought they were. We were close, or at least I believed we were. But then I started noticing things, little things that didn't add up. She and Adesh... they've been getting close, too close. And it's not just in my head, Sarthak. I've seen it- her actions, his behaviour. It's all there."

Sarthak listened intently, his expression concerned but neutral, giving Nahar the space he needed to express his feelings.

"I came on this trek hoping to clear my head, to figure out what the hell I'm supposed to do now. I thought maybe being out here, away from everything, would help. But every time I see them together... it's like a punch to the gut. And last night, when I saw them sleeping so close... it broke something inside me, Sarthak. I knew then that whatever we had, it's over. I just can't keep pretending anymore."

Nahar's voice cracked slightly as he continued, "I've been trying to hold it together, to not make a scene, to not let this ruin the trek for everyone else. But it's eating me alive. I don't know how to face her, how to face Adesh. I thought I could handle it, but being here, it's just made everything worse."

Sarthak put a reassuring hand on Nahar's shoulder, sensing the depth of his pain. "I'm really sorry you're going through this, Nahar. It sounds like you've been carrying this burden alone for too long. But I'm glad you told me. You don't have to do this alone anymore."

Nahar looked at Sarthak, grateful for his support. "Thanks, man. I don't know what I'm going to do, but at least now... at least now it's out there. I just need to get through the rest of this trek and figure out the next steps."

Sarthak nodded, understanding the gravity of the situation. "We'll get through this, Nahar. Whatever happens, I'm here for you. And if you need to talk more, or if you just want to get away for a bit, let me know. We'll figure it out together."

Nahar felt a small but significant sense of relief. He had finally opened up, and though the pain was still there, it was no longer something he had to carry alone. The trek had taken on a different meaning now-it wasn't just about reaching the peak anymore, but about finding a way to move forward, no matter how difficult that might be.

After their conversation, Nahar and Sarthak made their way back to the campsite. The rest of the group was already packing up, preparing for the final leg of the trek back to the village. The air was filled with a mix of excitement and nostalgia—everyone was eager to return to the comforts of home, but there was also a lingering sadness that the adventure was coming to an end.

As the group started the descent back to the village, Nahar and Sarthak hung back, walking at a slower pace than the others. The path was familiar now, winding through the same rugged terrain they had conquered just days before, but their journey was far from over. They walked side by side, their conversation picking up where it had left off.

"You know, Nahar," Sarthak began, his voice calm and reflective, "sometimes these experiences-like this trek-they're not just about the physical challenge. They're about what we learn about ourselves along the way."

Nahar nodded, his gaze focused on the trail ahead. "Yeah, I've been thinking about that a lot. This trek was supposed to be an escape, but instead, it's forced me to confront everything I've been avoiding. Maybe that's what I needed all along."

Sarthak glanced at him, his expression thoughtful. "Maybe. It's like the mountains—they're relentless, they push you to your limits, but they also have a way of showing you what really matters. You've faced some tough stuff, man, but you're still here, still moving forward. That says a lot."

Nahar smiled faintly, appreciating Sarthak's words. "I guess you're right. It's just... it's hard to see the bigger picture when you're in the middle of it all. But out here, with nothing but nature around us, it's like everything else falls away, and you're left with just your thoughts. It's both terrifying and liberating."

The two continued to walk, the village still a few hours away. The group ahead of them was becoming smaller in the distance, their voices faint echoes in the crisp mountain air. Nahar and Sarthak didn't mind the solitude—it gave them more time to talk, more time to process everything that had happened.

As they descended further, the scenery began to change. The snow-covered peaks gradually gave way to lush green valleys and dense forests. The crisp, cold air was replaced by the warmer, earthier scent of pine trees and fresh soil. The sound of their boots crunching on the snow transitioned to the soft rustling of leaves underfoot.

"Do you think things will be different when we get back?" Nahar asked, breaking the silence.

Sarthak shrugged, thoughtful. "Maybe. Or maybe not. But what's important is how you decide to handle it. You've been through a lot, but you're still in control of what happens next. Whether it's with Milli, with Adesh, or with anyone else-it's your choice."

Nahar took a deep breath, letting Sarthak's words sink in. "Yeah, I guess that's true. I just need to figure out what that choice is."

"You will," Sarthak replied with quiet confidence. "And whatever you decide, I'm here for you."

As they continued their descent, Nahar felt a sense of clarity starting to emerge. The path ahead might be uncertain, but he knew he wasn't alone. The trek had been challenging, both physically and emotionally, but it had also been a journey of self-discovery. And as they walked, side by side, he realized that maybe, just maybe, he was finally ready to face whatever came next.

After several hours of walking, the group finally reached the village in the afternoon. There was a sense of accomplishment in the air as everyone took their first steps back into civilization, their bodies sore but their spirits high. The village, with its modest houses and winding streets, felt like a warm embrace after the harshness of the mountains.

The group quickly gathered at a local eatery, where a simple but hearty lunch awaited them. Everyone ate in silence, the exhaustion of the trek settling in, but there was an underlying satisfaction as well. They had made it, together. The bond they had forged during the trek was evident in the small smiles and quiet conversations that passed between them as they ate.

As they finished their meal, Sikandar reminded them that the bus was waiting to take them back to the city. The realization that this was the final leg of their journey hit everyone. They gathered their belongings and made their way to the bus, each step feeling like they were leaving behind a piece of the adventure they had just experienced.

On the bus, everyone settled into their seats, the fatigue of the trek finally catching up with them. The mood was a mix of reflection and quiet chatter, with some people dozing off while others exchanged contact information, promising to stay in touch. Nahar and Sarthak sat together, their conversation from earlier still fresh in their minds, but they didn't say much, content to sit in companionable silence.

Chapter 32

The Last Night Together Unfinished Symphony

As the bus made its way through the winding mountain roads and back towards the city, the sky gradually darkened. Night fell, and the bus became quieter, the hum of the engine and the occasional bump in the road the only sounds breaking the silence. Nahar looked out the window, watching the silhouette of the mountains fade into the night, feeling a mix of melancholy and peace.

Hours later, the bus reached its final stop, a small town where Nahar, Sarthak, Adesh, Milli and two other members of the group were scheduled to get off. The six of them, the last of the group, gathered their bags and stepped off the bus. The town was quiet, with just a few streetlights illuminating the empty streets.

They decided to stay together for the night and found a nearby hotel where they could rest before parting ways the next day. The hotel was modest but comfortable, a welcome sight after days of trekking and a long bus ride. They checked in, found their rooms, and after dropping their bags, they all gathered in one room to share one last evening together. The conversation was light, filled with laughter and shared memories of the trek. They reminisced about the challenging climbs, wonderful views, and the rekindled friendship that had developed among them. Nahar felt a sense of contentment being with these people who had shared in his journey, both physical and emotional.

As the night grew late, one by one, they began to drift off to sleep, the fatigue finally overtaking them. Nahar lay awake for a few moments longer, reflecting on the trek and everything it had brought to light for him. He knew that the next steps in his life wouldn't be easy, but he felt more prepared to face them.

With that thought, he finally allowed himself to sleep, knowing that tomorrow would bring a new day, and with it, the start of the next chapter in his journey.

The next morning, after seeing off the two other members of their trekking group, Nahar, Adesh, Sarthak, and Milli decided to visit a nearby temple renowned for its ancient architecture. The temple stood as a majestic reminder of the past, with intricately carved stone pillars and an aura of tranquillity that seemed to seep into everyone who entered its sacred grounds. The group spent time wandering through the temple, admiring its beauty and soaking in the peaceful atmosphere.

Nahar found solace in the serene environment, allowing his mind to quiet for a while. The temple's grandeur and the spiritual energy it exuded made him reflect on the recent events, particularly the complex feelings he had towards Milli and Adesh. Despite the calm setting, there was a tension simmering beneath the surface, one that Nahar could not easily shake off.

After spending some time at the temple, they returned to their hotel room, aware that their train was scheduled for the night. The hotel room felt smaller than before, filled with the unspoken words and the weight of unresolved issues.

As they settled back into the room, Milli approached Nahar, her eyes searching for something in his expression. She stood close, her voice soft yet laced with an undercurrent of tension, as she asked, "Nahar, why are you keeping your distance from me and Adesh? Did we do something wrong?"

Nahar, who had been avoiding direct confrontation, tried to maintain a neutral tone. "No, I'm not keeping any distance from you," he replied, his voice steady but lacking the warmth it usually carried. He forced a smile, hoping to deflect the conversation, but internally, he knew the truth. He was keeping his distance, and it wasn't something he could easily explain without opening up wounds that hadn't fully healed.

Milli, sensing the disconnect, pressed further. "It feels different, Nahar. I don't want things to change between us."

Nahar looked at her, and for a brief moment, he saw the guilt in her eyes, the uncertainty that mirrored his own. He could see that Milli was trying to bridge the gap, trying not to be the villain in the story that had unfolded.

But Nahar also knew that some things couldn't be undone, no matter how much one wished they could be.

He took a deep breath, choosing his words carefully. "Things have been a bit complicated lately. Maybe it's just the exhaustion from the trek, or maybe… we just need some time to figure things out."

Milli nodded, but both of them knew that there was more to it than just exhaustion. The bond they once shared had been strained, stretched thin by unspoken truths and hidden betrayals. While Milli might have been trying to mend what was broken, Nahar wasn't sure if it could ever be the same again.

Adesh, who had been watching the exchange from across the room, stayed silent, sensing the gravity of the situation. Sarthak, too, noticed the tension but chose not to intervene, respecting the delicate balance of emotions in the room.

The day passed slowly as they waited for their train. There was a heaviness in the air, a shared understanding that something had shifted between them. Conversations were minimal, and when they did speak, it was mostly about mundane things-plans for the journey back, what they would do once they returned home-anything to avoid the real issues at hand.

As the evening approached and they prepared to leave for the train station, Nahar couldn't help but feel a sense of finality. The trek had been a journey of self-discovery, but it had also exposed the cracks in his relationships. He knew that moving forward would require more than just time-it would require facing the truth, however painful that might be.

As they left the hotel and headed to the station, Nahar remained lost in thought, contemplating what lay ahead. The train riding home would mark the end of one journey and the beginning of another-one where he would need to confront his feelings and decide how to navigate the complexities of his relationships with Milli and Adesh.

In the evening, they left the hotel room, the air filled with a sense of departure that was more than just physical. The trek, the temple visit, and the heavy conversations had all taken their toll. As they made their way to the railway station, the streets were bustling with activity, but within their group, the mood was quiet and reflective.

Nahar felt a deep sense of gratitude towards Sarthak, who had stayed by his side like a steady anchor throughout the entire journey. Sarthak's presence had been a constant source of support, especially in those moments when Nahar felt most vulnerable. Despite having only known each other for a short time, their bond had grown incredibly strong—a bond that Nahar hadn't managed to forge with Adesh, even after over a year of friendship.

As they arrived at the station, the familiar sounds of trains arriving and departing filled the air. The group gathered their bags and waited on the platform, the conversations kept to a minimum. Nahar felt a mix of emotions—relief that the journey was coming to an end, but also a lingering sadness for the strained relationships that had emerged during the trip.

When the train finally arrived, they boarded in silence, each finding their seats. Sarthak naturally took a seat next to Nahar, continuing to offer his quiet support. Nahar couldn't help but reflect on how much Sarthak had come to mean to him in such a short period. Their friendship felt genuine and effortless, a stark contrast to the complexities and unspoken tensions that now characterized his relationship with Adesh.

As the train began to move, Nahar looked out the window, watching the landscape slowly blur into the night. He was thankful for Sarthak's companionship, feeling a bond that was deeper than mere friendship—it was a connection built on trust and understanding, something Nahar had realized he had been missing with Adesh.

In the darkness of the train, with the rhythmic sound of the tracks beneath them, Nahar felt a sense of clarity. The journey had revealed the true nature of his relationships, and he knew that when they returned home, things would never be quite the same. But for now, he was content to sit in silence, grateful for the friend who had stood by him, helping him navigate through the emotional storm.

Nahar knew that whatever challenges lay ahead, he could count on Sarthak to be there, just as he had been throughout the trek. Their bond, forged in the mountains, would be something he would carry with him long after the journey ended.

After a quiet night dinner on the train, the group settled in for the journey. The rhythmic clattering of the train on the tracks seemed almost soothing to everyone but Nahar. While the others slowly drifted off to sleep, Nahar found himself wrestling with a storm of emotions inside.

He lay in his berth, staring at the ceiling of the compartment, the dim lights casting long shadows that seemed to mirror the heavy thoughts weighing on his mind. Every time he closed his eyes, the memories of the trek, the tension between him, Milli, and Adesh, and the newfound bond with Sarthak all came rushing back. The raw wound of betrayal still stung, and no matter how much he tried to push it aside, it gnawed at him, refusing to let go.

Nahar could feel the exhaustion in his body, the physical tiredness from the trek demanding rest, but his mind wouldn't cooperate. He kept turning over, trying different positions to get comfortable, but the restlessness persisted. His thoughts kept returning to Milli's question at the hotel, asking why he was distancing himself. He knew the answer, but saying it out loud would make everything too real, too painful.

Despite his best efforts to hold everything together, Nahar felt the cracks in his emotional Armor widening. He was broken inside, the weight of it all pressing down on him like a suffocating blanket. He wanted to cry, to let it all out, but he knew that wouldn't change anything. He felt utterly alone, even with his friends nearby.

Eventually, the exhaustion began to win out. His eyes grew heavy, and the thoughts swirling in his mind became less coherent. He wasn't sure when he finally fell asleep; it just happened, as if his body finally overruled his troubled mind. The sleep that took him was not peaceful, but it was a temporary escape from the overwhelming emotions that had consumed him.

In that fitful slumber, Nahar drifted, his dreams a tangle of unresolved feelings and half-formed images. The train continued its journey through the night, carrying him and his friends back to the life they had left behind, but for Nahar, the real journey was just beginning—a journey of healing and coming to terms with the painful truth that had surfaced during the trek.

As the morning light softly filtered through the train windows, Nahar slowly opened his eyes. The rhythmic motion of the train continued to lull most of the passengers into a deep sleep. Glancing around, he noticed that everyone else, including Sarthak, was still sleeping peacefully. The quietness of the compartment offered him a rare moment of solitude.

Nahar's seat was on the side lower berth, giving him a clear view of the landscape rushing by outside the window. He stretched slightly, feeling the stiffness in his muscles from the night before, and reached for the small bag of snacks he had kept nearby. As he nibbled on some biscuits, he plugged in his earphones, letting the familiar comfort of music envelop him.

The scenery outside was a soothing mix of early morning mist, lush green fields, and the occasional village. The sun was just beginning to rise, casting a golden hue over everything. The sight of nature in its raw, untouched form felt like a balm to Nahar's troubled mind. The music in his ears, combined with the peaceful view, provided a momentary escape from the turmoil he had been feeling.

With each passing minute, Nahar allowed himself to get lost in the melodies, the lyrics speaking to his heart in a way that words alone couldn't. The rolling hills, winding rivers, and endless stretches of fields seemed to flow in sync with the music, creating a perfect harmony that calmed him. For a while, he could almost forget the emotional weight he had been carrying.

But even in this peaceful moment, thoughts of Milli and Adesh occasionally surfaced. The pain wasn't gone-it was just held at bay by the tranquillity of the morning and the beauty of the world outside his window. Nahar knew that he still had a long way to go in coming to terms with everything, but for now, this quiet moment was enough.

As the train continued its journey, Nahar felt a small sense of hope. The world outside kept moving, and so would he. This moment, this morning, was a reminder that life had its own pace, and no matter how difficult things got, there was always the possibility of finding peace in the simplest of things-like the view from a train window, the taste of a snack, or the comfort of a song.

As the train continued its steady journey, Sarthak began to stir from his sleep. He rubbed his eyes, slowly becoming aware of his surroundings, and noticed Nahar sitting quietly by the window, lost in his own thoughts. There was a calmness in the way Nahar sat, his gaze fixed on the passing scenery, his earphones in, seemingly at peace.

Sarthak got up from his berth and walked over to Nahar, sitting down beside him without saying a word. For a moment, they both just sat there, silently sharing the view outside the window. Sarthak could sense the heaviness in Nahar's heart but chose not to press him with questions. Instead, he offered his silent support, his presence a reminder that Nahar wasn't alone in this.

A few moments later, Milli and Adesh began to wake up as well. They stretched and settled into their seats, slowly shaking off the remnants of sleep. The compartment was still quiet, with only the soft hum of the train and the occasional rustling of passengers waking up.

Milli's eyes drifted towards Nahar, who was sitting near the window with Sarthak by his side. Their eyes met for a brief second-a fleeting moment that seemed to stretch on longer than it actually was. Nahar could feel the weight of her gaze, and for a moment, it felt like all the unspoken words between them were hanging in the air.

But instead of holding that gaze, Nahar quickly turned his head back to the window, breaking the eye contact. He didn't want to confront those feelings right now, not in this confined space where there was no escape. The outside world seemed a much safer place to focus on, even if it was just a distraction.

Milli noticed the way Nahar turned away and felt a pang of guilt and sadness. She knew that things between them were not the same and that she was partly responsible for the distance that had grown between them. But she also knew that Nahar wasn't ready to talk about it, at least not now, and perhaps neither was she.

The silence in the compartment was thick with unspoken emotions. Sarthak, sensing the tension, stayed by Nahar's side, offering him quiet support. The train rolled on, carrying them all towards their destination, but each of them was lost in their own thoughts, the journey home now tinged with the weight of unresolved feelings.

As the landscape outside continued to change, so too did the dynamics within that small train compartment, where each of them was grappling with their own emotions in their own way. For now, though, they were all just passengers on a journey, moving forward, even if the path ahead was uncertain.

As the train neared Nahar and Sarthak's station, a quiet tension settled over the group. Everyone was in their own thoughts, the silence in the compartment reflecting the emotional distance that had grown between them. Nahar kept his eyes fixed on the passing scenery, using the view outside as a shield to mask the turmoil inside him. The familiar sights of the approaching station, usually a welcome sign of homecoming, now only added to the weight in his chest.

Nahar could feel the heaviness in his heart, a physical burden that made it hard to breathe. The emotional exhaustion of the trek and the unresolved tension with Milli and Adesh were taking their toll. But he was determined not to let it show. He had always been the one to hold things together, to appear strong even when he felt anything but. This moment would be no different.

He glanced briefly at Sarthak, who sat beside him, quietly supportive as always. Sarthak's presence was a comfort, a reminder that someone genuinely cared, even if words weren't exchanged. Nahar was grateful, but he couldn't bring himself to fully open up, not here, not now. Instead, he forced a small, almost imperceptible smile, trying to reassure Sarthak that he was okay, even though they both knew better.

Milli and Adesh were seated across from them, also lost in their own thoughts. Milli occasionally stole glances at Nahar, her expression a mix of concern and regret. She could sense his inner struggle, but like Nahar, she wasn't ready to confront it. Adesh, on the other hand, kept his gaze lowered, perhaps aware of the growing tension but unsure how to address it.

The train's slowing pace signalled that their station was close. Nahar took a deep breath, steeling himself for the moment when they would all have to disembark together. The idea of saying goodbye, even temporarily, felt heavy with the knowledge that things had changed between them, and not necessarily for the better.

As the train finally came to a halt, the usual flurry of activity as passengers gathered their belongings seemed muted. Nahar and Sarthak rose from their seats, collecting their bags in silence. Nahar's face remained a carefully composed mask, betraying nothing of the storm brewing inside. He made sure to keep his movements calm and deliberate, not wanting to draw any attention to his inner state.

As they stepped off the train, the cool air of the station hit Nahar's face, a small relief against the heat building in his chest. He glanced back at Milli and Adesh one last time before turning away, a silent goodbye that said more than words could. Sarthak was right beside him, a steady presence that Nahar could lean on, even if only for a little while.

The group began to part ways, each heading in their own direction. For Nahar, the weight in his chest remained, but he carried it with the quiet resolve that had seen him through so much before. This journey might be over, but the path ahead was still uncertain, and Nahar knew he had to face it, one step at a time.

As Nahar and Sarthak made their way off the platform, Nahar couldn't help but steal one last glance at Milli. She was standing at the train door, with Adesh beside her, both of them looking out as if searching for something-or perhaps someone. The moment their eyes met, Nahar felt a surge of emotions rush through him. But instead of finding solace, he felt an overwhelming sense of loss.

The weight in his chest grew heavier, and his head bowed slightly, as if the burden was too much to bear. He couldn't muster the strength to hold her gaze for long. It was as though every unresolved feeling, every unspoken word, had gathered in that single moment, leaving him emotionally drained.

Milli's face was a mixture of regret and sadness, a silent acknowledgment of the pain that lingered between them. Adesh, on the other hand, seemed caught between confusion and concern, perhaps sensing the depth of

Nahar's turmoil but unsure how to bridge the growing gap.

Nahar knew that looking any longer would only deepen the hurt. So, with a final, fleeting glance, he turned away, the image of Milli and Adesh standing together burned into his memory. It was a sight that he knew would haunt him for some time.

As Nahar and Sarthak began walking towards the exit gate, the sound of their footsteps echoed in the stillness of the station. Sarthak walked quietly beside him, his presence steady and comforting, yet the weight of the moment made each step feel like an eternity. The world around them seemed to move in slow motion, every detail imprinted in Nahar's mind-the dim lights of the station, the distant hum of voices, and the cool morning air that did little to ease the heaviness in his heart.

Nahar's thoughts were a tangled web of emotions—heartache, betrayal, and a deep sense of loss. He had come to this place hoping for closure, for some resolution to the conflicts within him, but instead, he felt more burdened than ever. The silence between him and Sarthak was thick with unspoken words, but it was a silence Nahar couldn't break, not yet.

As they passed through the exit gate, Nahar's heart felt heavier with each step. The realization that things would never be the same weighed heavily on him. He knew he had to move forward, but in that moment, all he could feel was the pain of what he was leaving behind.

Sarthak, sensing Nahar's inner turmoil, placed a comforting hand on his shoulder, a silent gesture of support that Nahar was deeply grateful for. They walked together, side by side, both aware that the journey they had just completed was more than just a physical trek—it was a passage through some of the most challenging emotional terrain Nahar had ever encountered.

As Nahar watched the train begin to pull away from the station, he felt an overwhelming finality settle over him. The sight of Milli, standing by the train door beside Adesh, was the last image he would ever have of her. It was a bittersweet moment, tinged with all the memories of their time together—the joy, the connection, and the pain that ultimately tore them apart.

The train's rhythmic clatter as it gained speed echoed the beating of his heart, a sound that grew more distant with each passing second, just like the memories of Milli that he knew would eventually fade into the past. Nahar stood still for a moment, watching as the train disappeared into the horizon, carrying away not just Milli, but the remnants of a chapter in his life that had now closed.

He knew that this was the end, that he would never see Milli again, and that the life they had shared, the dreams they had once nurtured together, were now just memories to be left behind.

As they exited the station, Nahar felt a strange sense of release. The weight that had burdened him for so long seemed to lift, if only slightly, as he stepped into the open air. The world outside was unchanged-life went on, as it always does, indifferent to the personal struggles that people carry within them.

Nahar and Sarthak hailed a cab that would take them home. The drive was quiet, with the city passing by in a blur of lights and shadows. Nahar leaned back in his seat, closing his eyes for a moment, letting the events of the past few days wash over him one last time. There was sadness, yes, but also a sense of acceptance. He had loved, he had lost, and now he had to move on.

When they finally reached Nahar's home, Sarthak gave him a firm handshake, a wordless promise of continued friendship and support. Nahar smiled weakly, appreciating the bond they had formed during the trek—a bond that would endure beyond the pain of the past.

Nahar walked into his home, the familiar sights and sounds greeting him like a comforting embrace. As he closed the door behind him, he knew that the journey he had just completed was more than just a physical one. It was a journey of the heart, a passage from one phase of life to another.

He set down his bag and looked around, the silence of the house a stark contrast to the emotional turbulence he had just endured. But in that silence, there was also peace—a peace that came from knowing that he had survived, that he had faced the pain head-on, and that he was now ready to let go.

Nahar took a deep breath, feeling the weight of the past slowly receding. He knew that the memories of Milli would always be a part of him, but they no longer had the power to hurt him. They were simply part of the story that had made him who he was.

And with that, Nahar moved forward, leaving the memories behind, ready to embrace whatever the future had in store for him.

And thus, their forever faded with no time in near future beyond their last kiss. The quiet divide brought a big gap between the two hearts.

Nahar, having walked on the path of love, loss, and self-discovery, finds himself at a new beginning. The echoes of the past, obsessively created by the two hearts which mistakenly considered love wasn't the love actually.

As **Smile Alys** quotes; *Obsession-It's not love. It's the most dangerous form of emotion which if not tamed can* *destroy everything around you, including you",* though poignant, no longer hold him captive. Instead, they become the foundation upon which he can build a new, carrying with him the lessons learned and the strength gained.

As Nahar closes this chapter of his life, the future remains unwritten, full of possibilities. The journey has shaped him, but it does not define him-what lies ahead will be his to create, with a heart that, though once broken, is now healing and ready for whatever comes next.

The train has left the station, the memories have been left behind, and Nahar stands at the threshold of a new dawn, ready to step forward into the light wherein he learned ***"The art of letting go"***

The End.

*"Love is like a butterfly;
it goes where it pleases,
and it pleases where it goes."*